D1409898

DOLPHIN DREAMS

**Center Point
Large Print**

**This Large Print Book carries the
Seal of Approval of N.A.V.H.**

DOLPHIN DREAMS

Annette Mahon

CENTER POINT PUBLISHING
THORNDIKE, MAINE

This Center Point Large Print edition
is published in the year 2008 by arrangement with
Avalon Books, an imprint of Thomas Bouregy & Co., Inc.

The text of this Large Print edition is unabridged. In other
aspects, this book may vary from the original edition.
Printed in the United States of America.
Set in 16-point Times New Roman type.

ISBN: 978-1-60285-130-6

Cataloging-in-Publication data is available from the Library of Congress.

For my writer friends, especially Terey, who believed in this book, and Shelley, who seems to like everything I write.

DOLPHIN DREAMS

Chapter One

Adam Donovan was *not* in a good mood. He'd had a busy day, much of it spent cooped up in offices talking to the resort management and bookkeepers, while outside the sun and the sea beckoned. The resort was an attractive property, but its financial situation was even worse than he'd been led to believe. It made him wonder if he'd been deliberately misled.

And now he was inside once again, at a reception for the groups that leased resort space to offer various activities to the guests. Adam frowned. He was the only one there in a suit and tie. His father insisted on formality during negotiations, even when they took place in informal areas. As Hawaii most definitely was.

The room was filled with young people, all tanned, buff, and healthy. Most of them would fit easily into an ad for Wheaties or a guest appearance on *Bay watch.* Under other conditions, Adam might have looked forward to associating with them. Today, however, he just wanted to be done with business, take a good long swim to get rid of the kinks caused by long distance travel and jet lag, then relax in bed with an old movie on the television.

He did, that is, until, from among the crowd of attractive outdoor types, one woman stood out. Trim and athletic, with dark wavy hair tumbling halfway down her back, she wore a slim red dress that skimmed her body, draping curves filled with promise.

It wasn't the color of her dress that drew his eye; many others in the room wore bright-colored clothes. She was laughing, as were others in her group. Yet he was sure that the musical sound wrapping itself around him belonged to her.

The woman's eyes met his, the contact holding for one brief moment. The laughter faded from her eyes and her expression sobered. A tightness clutched his chest before her eyes flickered away, back to the person with whom she was speaking. The fist in his chest loosened its hold and he breathed easily again.

The difficulties of the day fell away and Adam felt newly energized. The mere sight of the young woman in the red dress filled him with conflicting emotions.

A woman in a red dress was such a cliché. Yet there was something about her—an energy, a life force that emanated from her laughing face. His vision had actually blurred for a moment as though some mystic wave of energy passed between them.

Adam paused, irritated by the strange thought. If a friend had expressed such an experience to him, he would have dismissed it as a fanciful creation. Or asked how much his friend had had to drink. What to do when the fancy was his own? And he was stone cold sober.

As Adam worked to digest this new phenomenon, the resort's general manager appeared at his side— fawning, Adam noted with distaste. Still, he could use him to meet that interesting creature, no longer laughing but still part of a group. A group that now seemed to be debating something extremely serious, as half of them frowned unhappily.

It took mere minutes for Adam to steer the manager toward his target; another moment to learn the woman in red and her friends all worked for Dolphin Life Research, the organization that cared for the dolphins in their special lagoon—a big attraction for the resort. Excellent. The reception had been set up purposely so that he could meet this group in particular.

"And this is Jade Kanahele, our newest marine behaviorist."

Adam looked down into dark brown eyes, beautiful eyes tipped up at the outside edges and surrounded by lashes so lush and thick he felt sure she must get accused of wearing false ones. But he knew they were real, as real as those naturally pink-flushed cheeks. He'd seen artfully made-up women and he'd bet the Rolex his father gave him last Christmas that the only makeup she wore was the lipstick that stained her lips a deep plum.

Those lush lips smiled at him as she extended her hand, but he noted an apprehension in her exotic, cat-like eyes. He watched her lips move, thinking plum was a most attractive color, then realized she'd spoken to him and he hadn't heard a word.

He tuned back in to hear the manager speaking and decided he'd merely missed the kind of polite chitchat one said upon being introduced to a stranger. It was a shame, however, that he'd missed hearing her voice.

"Jade has just received her master's degree and will start working officially as a marine behaviorist tomorrow morning." The manager smiled benignly at her. "She has worked here part time over the years, though, so we're very happy to have her permanently."

Adam barely heard the gushing of the manager. He shook Jade's hand, continuing to hold it long past the time he should have released it. Her skin was warm, and as soft and smooth as a silken scarf. The energy he'd noted from across the room seemed to leap from her fingers into his palm, up his wrist and into his chest. Warmth sizzled through him, starting at their point of contact.

Pulling his hand reluctantly back to his side, he let his eyes travel slowly up her arm to her shoulder. To her long neck. Her skin was a beautiful golden brown and he desperately wanted to touch it again. How did she keep it so lovely when she spent so much time in the sun and salt water? He could still feel the smooth warmth of her hand, could imagine the silkiness of her cheek beneath his fingertips.

"I hoped to meet you all here this evening," Adam said, dragging his eyes from Jade's and forcing himself to acknowledge the others. For a moment, his eyes returned to Jade's face. Was it pure wishful desire, or was she staring at him too?

Adam had to concentrate to keep the conversation on track.

"I'm very interested in your dolphin program."

The marine biologists exchanged significant looks. Then a young man with California surfer looks replied. Ryan something. He wasn't usually so forgetful of names. It was important to know the names of possible future business associates.

"If you'd like to stop by the lagoon, we can show you what we do there."

"Could you tell me in general terms what programs you have for the hotel guests?"

Although he knew she was the newest hire, Adam's eyes went directly to Jade.

"There's a lottery held every day," Jade replied, "to choose the guests who will participate in swimming sessions with the dolphins."

"It's important for the health and well-being of the animals that they not be stressed by too much contact with humans," Ryan inserted.

"There are also special programs for children," Jade said.

There was more talk about what was available to the hotel guests, but the others gradually drifted off, each person making a polite excuse then leaving with a pointed look at Jade. Adam barely noticed. His attention was focused on Jade, a fact the others had obviously picked up and acted on. He wasn't unhappy by this, though he noticed some apprehension in Jade's eyes.

He didn't care. Close-up, her effect on him was devastating. Her exotic cat-like eyes smiled up at him and her lips moved. Once again he realized that he hadn't heard a word she'd said. And from her expectant look, she must have asked him a question and was awaiting a reply.

"I'm sorry."

The feel of her seemed imprinted on his hand from their brief handshake. Her warmth continued to sizzle through him, even now, so long after he'd released her hand.

Once more, his fingers twitched to touch her skin. Maybe later, he thought, his plans for a solitary evening rapidly changing. At the moment, though, he had to be the consummate businessman. He continued his apology.

"I'm afraid I was so caught by your lovely smile that I missed your question."

One of Jade's dark eyebrows arched upward. He liked her full eyebrows; he hated the way some women plucked them into thin unnatural lines. What that wickedly arched brow did to him . . .

But he'd better not think about it, not if he wanted to last the evening without embarrassing himself.

"Why don't we get a drink first?" he suggested.

He removed his hand from his pocket, and reached around her, escorting her toward a corner bar with a light pressure at her waist. The casual, polite gesture sent frissons of heat sparking through his system, surprising Adam. His fingers did not want to remain properly on her lower back. He'd never before realized how sensitive the pads of his fingers could be.

They made him aware of the silky smoothness of her dress, yet he could feel the heat of her skin beneath it as well. He wondered if she felt his hand tremble as he fought to control the impulse to trail his fingers up her back to the smooth bare skin of her neck. Around her throat then upward to her cheek.

Adam swallowed. Fine strands of hair brushed the back of his hand, adding to his discomfort. He took a deep breath and wondered why he was torturing himself. Perhaps he could suggest that they continue the party in his suite. What would her reaction be?

Her pleasant voice drew his attention back to the moment.

"Certainly, Mr. Donovan."

Suddenly, Adam felt old. "Please, call me Adam."

"Okay. Adam."

She smiled and he felt himself gripped by desire. The way she made him feel was far from old; he hadn't had such an intense reaction to a woman since his teenage years.

His name on her tongue sounded good. Real good. He stopped before the bar, relinquishing his hold on her waist. The simple action severed his connection with the energy that seemed to emanate from her, leaving him feeling cold and destitute.

To distract himself, he quickly asked her what she wanted, passing the request for ginger ale to the bartender. He got himself a Diet Coke. He liked to keep a clear head when discussing business matters. And Dolphin Life Research could play an important role in whether or not Donovan Enterprises decided to purchase and revamp the struggling Orchid House Resort.

Finally, moisture-beaded glasses in hand, he looked down at her and asked again about her earlier question.

Jade smiled and shrugged. "It seems silly now. I was just making conversation, asking how you liked the island."

He noticed that she refrained from asking how he liked the resort.

Her glance moved from him, roving quickly around the room then back again. She smiled sheepishly at him, looking up through the fringe of her lashes. His heartbeat accelerated at the disarming gesture.

Then she looked down, her attitude like that of a shy teenager. Adam wasn't sure if she was shy or embarrassed—or calculating. His initial impression was that she was no social sophisticate. She seemed to be all natural beauty and charm, from her unplucked eyebrows to her unpainted toenails peeking out from the low-heeled sandals on her feet. But truly unsophisticated women were hard to find these days. Women *pretending* naiveté on the other hand, were becoming increasingly common. And it was getting harder to distinguish between the two. He should know.

Tearing his thoughts from past unpleasantries, Adam replied to Jade's question about the locale. "I find the island beautiful. Definitely a paradise."

Jade nodded but did not smile. "The curse of the

islands, isn't it? A beautiful place to live, but one that everyone else wants to ravage."

Her eyes locked on his, and he had to reevaluate his initial impression of Ms. Kanahele. If she was socially unsophisticated, she was not inept at business matters. At least, he thought she was getting in a little dig about his interest in the resort, and her part of it.

Adam hid a smile. The last of his tiredness fell away. Here was an opponent worth engaging.

"Is that what you and your friends were discussing so seriously before I interrupted?"

Once again she nodded. "Dolphin Life Research does much more than provide the resort with dolphins to attract tourists. We do serious scientific work as well."

"Tell me about it."

And tell him she did. About the founders of Dolphin Life Research, a veterinarian and his animal behaviorist wife. About rescuing dolphins found injured in fish nets, or washed up on shore, then releasing them back into the wild. About breeding programs and research on dolphin pregnancies. About educating local school children on marine animals and how to treat and preserve them. It was obvious she felt a deep commitment toward dolphins and the work she did at Dolphin Life Research.

Finally, Adam began to feel that others in the room were staring at them. He'd been one-on-one with her for too long. The others must be wondering if he was talking business, or just hitting on her. Neither was good at this stage. So he let her move away and began to circulate.

It didn't take long before he found himself alone with another marine biologist. Tami was a tall blond with moss green eyes. She was toned and tanned, and older than Jade. Maybe older than Adam. She knew about relationships with men like Adam; he could tell by the way she cocked her head at him, and met his eyes boldly when their bodies "accidentally" brushed. So why didn't her body sliding against his create even half the sensation caused by a slowly arching eyebrow?

When she reached beyond him to set her empty glass on a tray and brushed his arm, Adam knew he was in big trouble. Because with an eager woman standing right beside him, Adam was more interested in the young, dark-haired beauty across the room.

Jade sipped her ginger ale while she listened with half her attention to one of the resort administrators expounding on the extra guests Dolphin Life Research could draw to the hotel if they would just let more people swim with the dolphins. This was exactly what the marine biologists at Dolphin Life worried about with the hotel for sale. Usually, Jade could declaim quite eloquently on this topic, but tonight she was distracted by Adam Donovan. Were the current managers feeling them out because that's what the potential buyer wanted?

Physically, she nodded her agreement with the statement Ryan had just made about the necessity of limiting the contact of wild creatures with humans. But her eyes continued to stray toward Adam, who was talking to Tami several feet away. He wore a sky-blue shirt with his tan suit; she'd noticed that it made his eyes look very dark. They were an incredible shade of blue, more like the deep ocean than the sky. Jade had always been partial to blue. It was her favorite color, had been since she was in kindergarten, maybe even before.

Quickly, Jade reminded herself of the impossibly corny response he'd made when his mind wandered at their introduction. Distracted by her lovely smile. Huh! Probably just thinking about how to get what he wanted from them all.

Before she got too fascinated by the handsome *haole*, Jade pulled herself back. If there was anything she hated in a man, it was that kind of smooth-tongued glibness. It reminded her too much of her last relationship. And she didn't want to think of that—or the man involved—again.

Just as she realized that she had completely lost track of the conversation, the doors to the adjacent room opened and everyone moved toward the buffet tables set up there. People immediately began to pass along both sides of the long tables, filling plates with the mouthwatering food from the sumptuous buffet.

"Do you think it tastes as good as it smells?"

Jade wasn't surprised to find Adam at her elbow. She seemed to be equipped with an Adam radar— some instinct had been at work all evening letting her know exactly where he was at all times. It was beyond incredible, but she had noticed that whenever the hairs on the back of her neck began to tingle, he appeared beside her.

She removed the hand that had been rubbing her nape and handed him a plate. "Only one way to find out." She took a plate for herself and started down the heavily laden table.

They moved down the line commenting on the various dishes, urging tastes to each other. Finally, Adam led the way to a table. Jade saw Tami wave at them, but he didn't appear to notice. He chose a spot two tables away, seating Jade between himself and the hotel general manager. The attractive Japanese woman sitting on the other side of Adam was an assistant manager.

Jade glanced at her table companions, looked down at her plate and felt her recently healthy appetite flee. Solid information had been hard to come by, but the hotel grapevine claimed that this get-together was to introduce a potential buyer to the parties who did business through the resort. That included most of the surfside businesses like boat rentals, canoe rides, snorkeling trips—and Dolphin Life Research. Dolphin Life Research might be considered an integral part of the resort, but they paid their rent like anyone else.

Tami had been with Dolphin Life Research for five years and said there had never been anything like it.

Everyone was aware the resort was not doing well. It was obvious from the number of empty rooms. And everyone seemed to know the hotel was for sale. Jade had certainly heard a lot about it when she'd stopped by over the weekend. That was also when she heard about the reception and been urged to attend. They had spent most of her visit debating the meaning and ramifications of the invitation. All of the groups present were separate entities from the hotel; but all, of course, were dependent on it.

And Adam Donovan was the guest of honor. No matter that he never quite disclosed his reason for being present. Everyone knew. Only someone in serious business negotiations with the resort would show up in a suit and tie.

Jade was finding her early pleasure in the invitation evaporating into a mist of concern. If the hotel sold, would the new owners honor the contract with Dolphin Life Research? If they did, would things remain the same? And how did Adam Donovan really feel about swim with the dolphins programs?

Despite her earlier concerns, Jade left the banquet hall with a smile on her face. Once past the early stress of meeting her bosses and the potential buyer's representative—not that anyone admitted that—the evening had been fun. With dinner, everyone relaxed. When the conversation turned to expanding the dolphin programs through education, she'd really begun to enjoy herself. One of Jade's favorite subjects, education was an area she was able to address with passion.

Her remembrance of Adam's face as he listened to

her discourse on dolphins brought a smile to her lips as she strolled from the room. He seemed every bit as enthusiastic as she was while he listened to her ideas on existing programs for school children and her proposals for the future. Anyone who was zealous about education could garner her approval.

"Ms. Kanahele? Is that you?"

The masculine voice startled Jade, making her start with surprise. Her hand went quickly beneath her hair to rub at that irritating prickling on her nape. That, and the tingly feeling shivering up her spine identified the speaker with the familiar baritone voice. Imagine, she didn't even have to see those amazing eyes for the man to have such an effect on her!

"Mr. Donovan." Jade turned to face him. "Are you making it an early night too?"

"Please, it's Adam, remember?"

Jade had to laugh. "Of course. I did remember, but I couldn't very well call you Adam when you'd just called me Ms. Kanahele, could I?"

Adam joined her laughter. She gazed into his eyes and felt much more comfortable around him than she had at the beginning of the evening. Perhaps because of their long conversation at the dinner table? Their long, *nonthreatening* conversation. Nonthreatening to her dolphins, at least, she thought, rubbing at her neck once again.

"You're right. And I didn't even realize I'd addressed you so formally."

"So, are you still jet-lagged?"

22

He raised a brow in her direction, which caused another shiver to pass through her. That one cocked brow, along with his stylish but disheveled hairstyle, gave him such a handsome look she felt he could compete with any movie star. She especially liked the way his squared jaw kept his face from being too pretty.

She watched his mouth move as he repeated her final words. He had a most attractive mouth.

"Jet-lagged?"

"You're retiring early," she reminded him.

Adam's lips curved into a beguiling smile. Jade caught her breath. Did she think he'd looked sexy before? The man smiling was a danger to womankind.

"No, I just thought it was time to go." His grin widened. "You know what they say about leaving them wanting more."

Jade smiled at his comment, but she had to force it. She was sure all the guests were sad to see him go. They had all been there to try and learn more about this man and his plans. From her own experience, she was sure no one had achieved any satisfaction. For a man who talked so much, he said surprisingly little about himself and his plans.

But now here he was. Perhaps she'd been given a second chance to learn something.

His next question brought her out of her reverie.

"What about yourself? Aren't you leaving rather early?"

Jade shrugged. "A working day tomorrow. My first day as an official marine behaviorist." This time she didn't have to force her smile. It came easily with her new job title. She'd waited a long time for this day.

Adam gestured down the hall, indicating that he would walk with her. They began to move toward the large double doors. "It's been a pleasure meeting you. I hope we'll see each other again."

Jade felt a shiver at his words. Was it her imagination, or did he infuse a sexual connotation into the simple phrases?

Jade reminded herself that this man could represent the next owner of the hotel, and that it was up to her to learn more about him and his plans. And that husky quality that made his words seem to mean so much more than the actual definitions might just be his natural way of speaking. Anyway, she would just take his words at face value, and reply to them as such.

"I enjoyed meeting you too. Will your business keep you here for long?" She was proud of the way she'd managed to insert that. He'd said very little about his job or his business at the resort. Anyone who questioned him directly received a cold look and an evasive answer. At least she avoided that. But she didn't get an answer either.

"Hard to say." He opened the door for her, following her out onto the hotel grounds.

"You don't have to go any farther with me," Jade told him as she stepped outside. She had a feeling that letting him know she didn't expect his escort was the certain way to ensure it. And for now, she wanted to keep him as a friend. "I'm parked in the employee lot.

It's on the other side of the gardens, and I'm sure it will take you out of your way."

Her gamble paid off. Adam wasn't to be persuaded away.

"It's a beautiful night. I'd enjoy the walk. I'd hoped to get in some swimming before bedtime, but it's a little late now. The pool will be closed. A long walk will be almost as good."

Jade took in a lungful of the fragrant night air. Low lamps lit the paths through the extensive gardens, and the numerous flowering plants lent their perfume to the night. Ocean waves broke on the nearby beaches, adding their soothing lullaby to their walk.

Adam placed his hand on the small of Jade's back. He just meant to guide her forward on the narrow path, but he felt her body tremble at his touch. She didn't say anything, or give any other clue that his presence affected her. He smiled. So the cool Ms. Kanahele wasn't as impervious as she tried to make out. The chemistry between them was so charged it had seemed impossible that only he could feel it.

"It's a beautiful night." Adam looked upward, though he continued to follow Jade. "The stars always seem brighter in the tropics."

"No air pollution," Jade pronounced. "Probably less light pollution too."

Adam laughed. "So unromantic of you. Shouldn't you have said it was because the stars *are* brighter here, or that the sea air and warm breeze just make them seem more beautiful?"

"I guess I'll have to allow you to be the romantic one. I'm a scientist, remember?"

Adam was brought up short by her statement. He'd always considered himself a scientist as well. Or rather, of a scientific bent. How could he now be the romantic one?

Whatever, he must be losing his touch. Women usually reacted in a much warmer manner to him. More in the way of the luscious Tami. He might not have been interested in her silent proposition, but it bothered him that Jade seemed so completely indifferent to him.

She did, however, stop and turn when she realized he was no longer with her. One arched brow reached up toward her hairline, and Adam swallowed hard.

"Is something wrong?"

Yes, Adam thought. *Something is definitely wrong.* But he couldn't very well tell her that his reaction to her was out of line for a man his age. He was behaving like a sixteen-year-old.

He thought quickly to provide a reason for his stop. Something other than the truth.

"I was just wondering if you didn't feel cold in that dress."

If possible, her brow moved even higher. And her voice almost had *him* shivering with cold.

"I suppose you were going to offer me your jacket," she said.

"No." He offered a slow smile that she could interpret as teasing. "But I could."

An interesting combination of warmth and ice was

his response. One moment she was all friendly smiles, the next she looked ready to punch him out. A fascinating puzzle.

Then she seemed to achieve a certain control. The friendly smile returned, but there was no sparkle in her eyes.

"Thank you for the sacrifice, but I'm fine. We're almost there."

Jade walked forward once more, gesturing toward the as yet unseen parking lot.

"Already?"

He could see Jade bite her lip as though uncertain of speaking. Or perhaps deciding on just what to say.

"The gardens are lovely."

For the first time, Adam looked around him. "I haven't had a chance to see them." Real regret came through in his voice. "I like gardens."

His simple statement drew a glance of both surprise and approval from his companion. It also brought them up to an *'ohi'a lehua* hedge. Through the moon-silvered leaves and the spiky red blossoms, he could see numerous parked cars. With deep disappointment, he realized they must have reached the employee parking lot.

Jade's words confirmed it.

"Well. Here we are."

Did Jade seem nervous? Adam wondered. Did she think he was going to attack her? Or perhaps just kiss her silly? Not that he wasn't tempted. But he had a lot more business to conduct at the Orchid House resort.

He couldn't let adolescent hormones sidetrack him.

He took her hand. It was small in his, her fingers long and slender. Irrelevantly, he wondered if she played the piano.

"It's been a real pleasure, Jade. I hope we'll meet again soon."

Jade smiled nervously at him, mumbling something suitable that he barely heard. He was more interested in her apparent confusion. He wished he'd taken her hand earlier. He had a feeling Ms. Kanahele might be as affected as he was by raging hormones.

Suddenly, Adam knew that Jade expected him to steal a kiss. But he enjoyed doing the unexpected. So he escorted Jade to her car and wished her good night.

Then he stood in the moonlight smiling, as she fumbled with her keys and headlights before backing up and driving away.

Chapter Two

As she drove home, Jade tried to evaluate her time with Adam. He'd been a proper businessman mixing with the crowd at the reception. But when they were alone together she felt certain he'd been flirting. In fact, she'd held her breath when they reached her car, fearful that he meant to steal a kiss. Then found herself disappointed when he didn't even try. Even more so when she realized how little she knew about him and the reason for his presence at the resort.

After dinner, he'd participated in a long discussion

on educating people, especially children, about the ocean and environmental issues, including dolphins. But on the whole, she'd learned nothing at all from him. Not whether he really was looking into purchasing the resort. Not whether his company would be willing to allow Dolphin Life Research to continue as it was, or whether they would want to expand the swim with the dolphins program. Not even the name of the company he represented.

Jade sighed in frustration. Adding to her annoyance was the fact that although he projected an air of arrogance and eliteness particular to the rich, she was inexplicably drawn to the man. Hadn't she learned *anything* from her last disastrous relationship?

Of course, Adam was incredibly good-looking, but she wasn't so shallow that looks alone would attract her. There was something strangely physical that happened to her whenever he was around her. She didn't understand it, but it was there. And caused some very odd—though not unpleasant—sensations.

The words *strange* and *odd* brought to mind a conversation Jade had with her mother the afternoon before. Odd and strange played a large part in that too. Also, the suggestion of a new relationship.

She'd been in her bedroom checking to be sure she had everything she would need in her new home when her mother walked into the room, a large sheet-wrapped bundle held in her arms.

"I wanted you to have this before your big day tomorrow."

"Is it a quilt?" Jade's voice rose in excitement as she reached over to touch the muslin-covered bundle held securely in her mother's arms.

"This, Jade, is our legacy."

Startled by the deep solemnity of this statement, Jade's hand fell back to her side. She stared at her mother. "Our legacy?"

Carol nodded. "The legacy of the Lovell family women."

Jade's eyes widened. The Lovells were her ancestors on her mother's side, several generations back. They had Lovell cousins.

"This is a very special gift, Jade. I hope it will mean as much to you as it always has to me." Her light chuckle softened the somber mood. "Of course, I didn't appreciate it right away. It took time and contemplation before the meaning became clear."

Usually a very straightforward woman, her mother's suddenly obscure conversation puzzled Jade.

But Carol was very good at reading her daughter's mind. "I'm not crazy." She smiled. "Or getting sloppily sentimental in my old age."

Carol placed her bundle on the bed and parted the muslin. As she turned aside the protective sheet, yellowing fabric covered with tiny stitches began to appear.

"It *is* a quilt! Is it one of Grandma's?"

There was excitement in Jade's voice. Her Grandmother Lucas made wonderful Hawaiian quilts, presenting each of her grandchildren with a quilt when they graduated from high school.

"Ah, this one is even better than one of Grandma Lucas'." Carol's hand ran gently over the beautiful stitching. "Help me lay it out so that you can see."

Reverently, the two women unfolded the old quilt, laying it out on Jade's bed. The fabric was old, the red of the design slightly faded, the white of the background yellowing.

In classic Hawaiian style, the quilt design was created like a giant paper snowflake. Folded and refolded, the pattern was cut from the large fabric triangle formed, thereby creating a unique repeating design, eight times over. The old quilt was large enough to cover a double bed to within an inch of the floor.

"Oh!" Jade let out her breath in a long, reverential sigh. "Oh, Mom, it's beautiful!"

The red fabric branched out across the white, the result a lacy pattern of leaves and flowers. The stitching was exquisite, defining the petals of the flowers and the veins of the leaves, then echoing out across the white like the ripples of ocean waves. A scalloped border in the red fabric framed the whole, a further reflection of the ocean waves that surrounded the island.

"It is beautiful, isn't it?" Carol examined the quilt as greedily as Jade. "It's been a long time since I've seen it laid out this way." She put her arm around Jade's shoulders and squeezed.

Jade leaned closer. Her fingers skimmed over the surface of the quilt; she was almost afraid to touch it.

"It looks very old. Like it should be in a museum."

"Maybe it should be." Carol blinked, her eyes damp with emotion. "This quilt was made back in 1915 by Helen Lovell, Grandma Lucas' grandmother."

"My great-great-grandmother?" Jade's eyebrows flew upward and her voice lowered in awe as she stuttered over the "greats."

"It's too bad we couldn't have known her." Carol sighed. "She must have been a wonderful woman. And so much in love with her husband. She's a legend in our family, you know."

"A legend? How come I've never heard about her?"

Carol met her daughter's eyes, managing to make Jade feel guilty with that one look.

"Because you young people are so busy nowadays that you don't have the time or inclination to learn about genealogy."

Jade really felt guilty now. Genealogy was an important part of her Hawaiian heritage. Before they had a written language, a designated family member would spend hours learning genealogy, long strings of names memorized and passed on. With today's computers, genealogy was so much simpler. Perhaps now that she was done with her degree, she could take some time to learn more about her ancestry.

Carol took Jade's hand and held it, cradling it between both of hers.

"Helen Lovell was married at eighteen, to a young man who worked for her father. His name was Thomas Keahi. Her parents didn't want her to marry.

She was young, and hadn't known Thomas for very long. But she was very sure of her love, and of Thomas' love."

Carol paused for a moment. Jade was fascinated. Apparently, her education about her family would begin immediately. Over the years, she had heard tales of her parents' wonderful marriage—and her grandparents' too. There was a tradition in the family that claimed their women were experts at finding good men.

"The Lovells had a large and successful ranch in Waimea. They were an important family in the area, social and political leaders. Helen's mother was descended from one of the great island chiefs, and her father from one of the island's first missionary families. Helen was their youngest child."

Carol paused, while Jade waited anxiously for the story to continue.

"Thomas, on the other hand, came from a large family who'd worked for the Lovells for many years. The men were *paniolos,* and the women often cleaned or cooked for the Lovells. I think part of her parents' dissatisfaction with Helen's choice was the fact that they felt she was marrying beneath herself. That kind of thing was important in Victorian times."

Carol paused again, looking to Jade as though expecting a comment. Jade nodded her understanding. Satisfied, Carol continued.

"But they loved their daughter, so Helen and Thomas were married."

Carol's voice became thicker as she progressed through the tale. It was such a lovely story, Jade was surprised she hadn't heard it before.

"Helen may have already been pregnant when she married." A quick grin touched Carol's lips. "They didn't like to talk about things like that back then, tried to keep it quiet when it did happen. But if she wasn't pregnant for the ceremony, then she quickly became pregnant with my grandmother, Valerie. There must have been a lot of talk at the time because Valerie was born exactly eight and a half months after their wedding day."

Things hadn't changed too much, Jade thought. People would still talk today, even though many people lived together for years without marrying. Yet there remained some strange compulsion among friends and relatives to count up the months between weddings and births.

"Helen didn't feel well while she was pregnant—she didn't just have morning sickness, she was ill the whole time. The baby was small and probably early. We're all lucky that baby survived," Carol added with a rueful smile. "Otherwise none of us would be here."

Carol folded up the end of the quilt, motioning Jade to join her in sitting at the end of the bed. Jade helped her readjust the old quilt so that there would be enough space for them to sit on the plain bedspread beneath. Hawaiian quilts were not sat upon; it was disrespectful to the person who made it.

Once again, Carol took hold of her daughter's hand.

She seemed to need the physical contact while she told her story.

"As I said, Helen felt ill throughout the pregnancy but she and Thomas were both thrilled about the baby. To keep busy, she began a quilt. She had learned how to make them with her mother and her aunts, but had never made one all by herself. But she was determined to make this quilt alone."

Carol squeezed Jade's hand. She turned toward her, looking deeply into her daughter's eyes.

"You know that we Hawaiians believe that the stitcher imparts her soul into her quilt—her *mana.*"

Jade nodded. She was interested in traditional Hawaiian crafts, and since there had always been quilters in her family, Jade knew a lot about quilting. She meant to try it herself someday.

"Helen worked very hard on this quilt, at a very important time in her life. She designed it herself, using leaves and flowers from her gardens for the pattern. She chose the scalloped border to indicate the ocean waves that surround the island. She spent every spare moment working on it, from the time immediately after her wedding, right up until Valerie was born."

Carol bowed her head. "Sadly, Helen never recovered from the birth. She died when Valerie was less than a year old."

Jade felt hot tears dampen her eyes at the thought of her great-great-grandmother never knowing her child; and of the child, her great-grandmother, who had never known her mother.

Carol continued, her voice husky with emotion. "My mother, and I myself, believe that this quilt is filled with Helen's *mana,* her love and her belief in romantic love. It's a powerful *mana.* And because of it, the quilt has a special ability to impart this love and belief in love to its owner."

Still thinking of the sad story she'd just heard, Jade blinked at her mother in confusion.

"You believe what?" Surely she misunderstood. Had her mother suggested that the beautiful quilt was similar to a love potion?

Carol dropped her daughter's hand, after giving it another affectionate squeeze.

"I don't expect you to understand. Yet. But you take my word for it, this quilt is very special. And for more reasons than just its beauty."

Skeptical of her mother's last words, Jade ignored them.

"I love it! Do you know what this pattern is called?"

"Helen called it *Ka Makani Ka'ili Aloha.* It means 'The wind that wafts love from one to another.' "

Jade sighed. "That's beautiful."

"Helen's parents took in the motherless baby, and between Thomas and her grandparents she heard all about her mother. Thomas kept the quilt—it was very special to him. He told his in-laws that when he slept under it, Helen visited his dreams. During one of these dreams, Helen told Thomas to give the quilt to Valerie when she finished school and was old enough to be married. I don't think he would have parted with it otherwise. Helen was his one true love; he never remarried."

Carol and Jade stood for a moment, her last words, related in a quiet voice, filling the air between them still.

"So Thomas gave the quilt to his daughter when she graduated from high school. She married—less than a year later. She gave it to her daughter at her graduation, and she too married within a year. Grandma Lucas gave it to me when I finished my nurse's training. I met your father my first day at work. And now it's time for me to pass it on to you."

Jade hugged her mother, placing a kiss on her cheek. "*Mahalo.*"

The softly spoken word lingered in the air between them, a special thank you from the younger generation to the older.

As she stepped back, Jade's eyes eagerly sought the quilt once more. "It's so beautiful. I will feel honored to have it in my new home."

She decided to disregard her mother's implication that owning the quilt would provide her with a husband. Within a year.

Back home after the reception, Jade turned down her new quilt, thinking again of her mother's strange ideas about it. And her own even stranger reaction to Adam Donovan. There couldn't be a connection, could there?

Dismissing such ridiculousness with a laugh, Jade

smoothed the quilt and reached for the sheet. Just thinking of Adam brought his image to life. She couldn't help wondering if perhaps he was settling into his own bed at that moment.

Blushing furiously at the warmth that spread throughout her body at the thought, Jade took a heavy tome on dolphin behavior off her shelf and brought it back to the bed. The old textbook was so dull, reading it for a while would probably put her right to sleep.

Jade adjusted the covers, watching Hina, her gray tiger cat, leap onto the bed and search for a comfortable sleeping spot. She'd noticed that Hina did not sleep, or even walk, on the old quilt that now covered her bed. Somehow, the cat seemed to know that the quilt should be treated with respect. The humid Hawaiian atmosphere was hard on textiles, so antique quilts were to be treasured. But how did Hina know how precious it was?

Jade glanced fondly at the red and white quilt she'd folded carefully at the bottom of the bed. She treated it with the utmost care, even though she didn't credit her mother's strange notion about the quilt bringing her true love.

Jade was still shaking her head over the incredible story when she climbed beneath the sheet and opened her book.

In what seemed no time at all, her eyes drooped closed.

And then the alarm was ringing.

Jade awoke suffused with happiness and peace. Not

the joyous anticipation she'd felt for the past week, when she'd been looking forward to her new job. This was an inner harmony, a spiritual comfort.

She lay in bed, her eyes wide open, her hand absently patting Hina who was curled on the pillow beside her head, as she tried to find a reason for the special serenity she felt.

Her lips parted in a blissful smile when she realized the source of her new inner harmony. She'd dreamed of dolphins! She'd been swimming in the ocean, and a pod of dolphins had come to join her. They swam all around her, communing with one another through their unique echolocation clicks. In the dream, she could feel the strange tingling as the sonar passed over her, followed by the most wonderful feeling of comfort and support.

With a blissful smile, she jumped out of bed, startling poor Hina who ducked beneath it.

Reaching to straighten the bedclothes, Jade saw that she'd pulled the old quilt up over her during the night. She'd have to be more careful. Still, the quilt was okay, the sky outside her window was clear and blue, and she was an official marine biologist at Dolphin Life Research. Life was beautiful.

Jade crossed the wooden bridge trying unsuccessfully to hide an ever widening grin. It didn't seem professional, somehow, coming to work with an asinine grin splitting her face. But, darn, she was happy. Many of her friends were still living at home, still sending out resumés.

Many more were staying on the mainland where they'd gone to school, complaining about the lack of jobs in the islands, hoping to return soon. And here she was, with a great family, a lovely condo, a beautiful antique quilt covering her bed, and a dream job working with her favorite animals. What more could a girl want?

A man.

The thought whispered through her mind, carried on angel's wings. Startled, Jade paused mid-step. The brief words were so real it was almost as if someone had spoken them aloud, softly, somewhere in the vicinity of her right ear.

Completing her interrupted step, Jade paused to glance around her. People filled the area, staff and guests both. Yet it took mere seconds for Jade's eyes to slam up against a pair belonging to a man sitting at the farthest table of the snack bar.

Adam! He sat alone, casually taking in his surroundings as he sipped from a cup of what she assumed was coffee.

Separated by some twenty feet, Jade still felt a strange twist in her chest, a knot in her gut, and the sudden absence of breathable air. As she wondered if she could be having a sudden allergic reaction, she felt the sea breeze ruffle her hair and once more thought she heard the words "a man."

Her eyes widened in surprise as they lingered on those eyes in the near distance. Even from her place on the bridge, she could see the blue of his eyes. As blue as the Pacific ocean.

He nodded at her, and the small acknowledgment broke the moment of suspended animation. Jade took in a deep lungful of healthy sea air, returned his nod, and continued her journey across the bridge.

She would not ruin this wonderful day by thinking of Adam Donovan and his business activities. Of the possibility that even now, he might be planning brochures touting the health benefits of swimming with the hotel's friendly dolphins. Could it be a coincidence that he sat in the snack bar overlooking the dolphin lagoon?

But she soon realized telling herself she would not think of Adam Donovan wasn't enough to banish him from her day. Tami and Ryan were anxious to compare notes from the previous evening and talk about the hotel's future. They too saw him at the café overlooking the lagoon.

"I guess there's no question that the hotel is for sale?" Jade asked.

Ostensibly, they were readying things for the morning programs. Jade held a clipboard listing upcoming school visits, Tami checked life vests and masks for the morning swim session, and Ryan was playing with the dolphins by tossing a ball for them to retrieve.

Ryan answered Jade's question with a shake of his head. "You won't get any of the managers to say so outright, but I've been told it is—unofficially." He took the ball back from Lae'ula as he spoke, offering her a small fish as a reward.

"I did an online search last night," Tami told her. "Adam is the son of Warren Donovan, CEO of Donovan Enterprises. They own several resorts, all top of the line, and all located in warm climates. There are several in the Caribbean and others in Mexico, Florida, and southern California. So far, they don't have a place in Hawaii."

"They're a solid company," Ryan continued even as he threw the ball across the water once again. "They haven't built too quickly like many do. That's when they tend to spend too much and then have to sell or go bankrupt. They like to find a place that's not doing well, take it over and revamp it."

Jade didn't need a map to direct her. Even without Ryan's unofficial confirmation, everyone was aware of the high number of empty rooms. "A place like the Orchid House."

All three were silent for a moment. It was good that such an upright company was interested in the hotel, but they had other issues on their minds.

Tami left the life jackets and joined Jade and Ryan on the deck. "Did you notice how many questions he had about Dolphin Life Research?"

There was no doubt in anyone's mind who she referred to with her "he."

"Does Donovan Enterprises have any hotels that offer swimming with dolphins?" Jade asked.

Ryan and Tami exchanged a look. Jade sometimes felt left out when she was with them. They had worked together for a long time and seemed able to communicate with little more than looks. Although she had no firm basis for the thought, she sometimes wondered if they had ever been more than just friends.

Jade pushed the idea from her mind. They couldn't have. It would make it impossible to work together, wouldn't it?

Dismissing such speculation, Jade fixed her mind on her question about dolphin programs.

Tami nodded, her lips tight. "There's a Donovan resort in Florida that has a program."

"Though, to be fair," Ryan inserted, "that hotel has been offering the program for years. Donovan Enterprises just bought them two years ago." While he spoke, he tossed the red ball far out into the lagoon. Once again, Lae'ula raced after it.

Jade bit her bottom lip, her eyes following the sleek animal. "But they're still doing it?"

Tami nodded. "If Dolphin Life allowed it, I'm sure the Orchid House would bring in anyone who wanted to swim with our dolphins. It's a sure moneymaker. So far we've been able to hang on to the research label, but I don't know if we can do it forever."

"We don't have to tell you how that kind of activity would interfere with our research. Even though we do these short swim sessions here, they're nothing like what some of the other resorts offer."

All three frowned.

Jade groaned. "And poor Lae'ula pregnant too."

Her eyes turned toward the lagoon where Lae'ula had just surfaced, the red ball bobbing on the water beside her. With a quick dip and flip, she sent the ball sailing through the air, straight toward Ryan and the others.

"Why wasn't Dr. Hobson or his wife there last night?" Jade asked. Dr. Raymond Hobson, a marine mammal veterinarian, was the founder and head of Dolphin Life Research. He taught at the university on Oahu and supervised the DLR program at a resort there as well as this one on the Big Island. His wife, Dr. Victoria Jones-Hobson was a dolphin behaviorist and worked closely with him. "Shouldn't they have been there to defend our program?"

"I don't think there was enough time for him to adjust his schedule and make the arrangements. They just issued the invitations the day before, remember?"

"I guess." Jade knew Tami was right. She was only able to attend because of her timely visit.

Jade moved her foot through the water, hardly aware of what she was doing. It would be terrible if she lost her job when she'd barely even begun. She wouldn't be able to compromise her principles and work at the resort if they didn't keep the dolphins in a proper environment. Though she did feel that Dr. Hobson would close Dolphin Life rather than submit to blackmail to keep the facility open.

She heaved a sigh. "I hope things stay the same."

"Don't we all," Tami agreed.

Ryan picked up the ball and tossed it again. "Amen."

Jade kicked her bare foot through the water, flicking

droplets of water several feet in front of her. Laka swam over to have a look, her year-old baby at her side. The two of them floated nearby, their foreheads visible, the rest of their bodies suspended just below the surface. The sound of their breathing brought a comfortable feeling to Jade. This had to work out right, she thought, as she looked into Laka's warm brown eye. Her *'aumakua* would see to it.

Chapter Three

Throughout the day, Jade was haunted by quick visions of Adam's handsome face. By blue eyes as clear as the west Hawaii sky. By—most distracting of all—wide firm lips, offset by a square jaw, and parted in a friendly smile. A slightly crooked smile, filled with promise.

No matter how often she scolded herself, Jade's heart skipped a beat each time his image appeared in her mind, a hazy vision floating through her thoughts.

The tenth time Jade envisioned that smile—while she was explaining to a group of young children what foods dolphins ate—an almost electric tingle raced up her spine. Instinctively, her eyes moved upward and her gaze clashed with that of her would-be nemesis. Dark eyes met pale blue ones.

Her heart almost ceased beating, and Jade lost her train of thought. She stopped speaking and glanced at the children, then at the dolphins watching them from the water, then at the bucket in her hands. Ah, food.

The moment of panic passed as she recalled what she'd been saying and was able to continue.

"Dolphins eat many different kinds of fish. They also eat squid and shrimp."

Jade could no longer see Adam, but she could feel his presence behind her, as strange as that seemed. The whole day was taking on a dreamlike quality that was rapidly heading toward nightmare.

Jade led the children closer to the water, showing them how to enter the pool, then how to put their hands in the water to greet the dolphins. Despite the cool water of the lagoon, Jade was feeling warm. And there was a strange tingle at the base of her neck and a roiling in her stomach that she suspected was an indication of stress.

Her mind refused to stay on her work. There he was, in the flesh, standing beyond the barrier, watching her. What was he doing there? Planning ways to sabotage their business? Imagining new programs dictated by the hotel?

Jade angled her body to the right. She had to get Adam out of her sight before she mangled her presentation and lost her dream job on the first day. And then how would she meet the payments on her wonderful condo? He could cost her her entire dream for the future!

Jade moved the children farther into the water, continuing to speak.

"I'm going to give you each a fish now, so you can feed the dolphins later. You give it to them head first," she added, showing them how to tuck the fish into the life vest's straps for easy access later.

Jade moved along the line, giving each child a fish. She liked talking to children, loved sharing her knowledge of her favorite animals. She couldn't allow Adam to ruin her dream job if his father decided to buy the hotel.

Was it any wonder her tummy was doing back flips?

So how could she get him over to her side?

Adam stood near the dolphin pool watching the employees of Dolphin Life Research work with a group of children. Jade and Tami were in the water, and he couldn't help but notice how delighted Jade seemed at every interaction with the children.

Adam recalled his first sight of her that morning, poised on the short wooden bridge that crossed the dolphin pool. Clad in a deep blue swimsuit and a pair of tan shorts, she was slim, athletic, and graceful. Happiness radiated from her, and her step had a bounce to it that made him feel she would rather run or skip along the path than walk like a mature adult. Her suppressed energy sprang across the bridge, over the rail, and into his chest.

Perhaps it was the obvious joy that emanated from her. Everyone she passed smiled to see her. She looked like someone enjoying her first Hawaiian vacation, not a hard-working scientist. Even now, near the end of a long hot day, an aura of cheerful enthusiasm permeated the area around her.

Adam had to admire anyone who could show such enthusiasm for her job. He wondered how many people did so. If he went out on the street and stopped a hundred people, how many of them would say they loved their jobs? Fifty percent? Twenty-five? Ten?

Adam shook his head. When had he become such a cynic? He enjoyed *his* job. He was going to be thirty years old next week, and he'd already gained a reputation for his ability to find good properties ready for acquisition. And then turn them around. He was the envy of men twice his age.

He'd been working for Donovan Enterprises since his high school years. He began at the resort in Florida where they lived—the first Donovan resort property. Although his father founded the corporation and retained controlling interest, Adam started in minor jobs, working his way up as he acquired more education and experience.

In the last few years he'd been scouting out properties for them to buy. It turned out he was very good at it. So far, all his recommendations had performed just as he'd suggested they would.

So why was he staring at the dolphin pool, wondering about job satisfaction?

Like the irresistible song of the Sirens, Jade's presence at the dolphin lagoon had lured him the entire day. Luckily, he'd had business to attend to that morning, meetings that stretched out past the lunch hour. But now, in the sultry heat of the tropical afternoon, he'd finally given in. He'd changed out of his formal clothes, opting for a polo style shirt and khaki shorts. He'd meant to observe all the trainers and watch their interaction with the children and the dolphins. The dolphin program was a prime attraction at the resort and he wanted to see exactly what was involved in the limited swim with the dolphins program they offered.

Yet, again and again, Adam found his eyes drawn to Jade. Small and slim, she had a perfect oval face, and large dark eyes filled with delight. Whether her happiness came from the children or the dolphins, he couldn't say, but she appeared to be a woman who loved her job.

And Adam was undeniably interested in her; there was some unseen connection between them that he wanted to explore.

The obvious attraction between them had him wondering if it was just time to pursue another relationship. Adam had not been involved with anyone since he'd discovered the gold-digger propensities of his last girlfriend over the holidays. More than six months had passed with no serious interaction between himself and a member of the opposite sex.

Adam frowned as Jade turned so that he could no longer see her face. Not that the view was any worse. She had a great figure whether viewed from the front or the back or the side—none of it hidden by the one-piece swimsuit she wore. A long, dark braid trailed down her back; fine tendrils of curly hair escaped its confines along its length, tempting his fingers to reach out and release the lot.

As Adam attempted to curtail his active imagination, he saw her glance quickly toward him, then just as quickly turn away. She led the children into the water, farther from his vantage point, talking all the while.

A sudden smile secured him favorable glances from several women nearby. Not that he noticed. His full attention remained on the shapely marine biologist. She was scarcely larger than the children she directed, but all woman. And she was trying to avoid him! He'd bet on it. He recognized evasive techniques. Not that they were often practiced on him. No, *he* was usually the one trying to avoid a clingy woman, or seeking to evade one becoming too serious. Quick glances and subtle turns to avoid eye contact—exactly what Jade was now doing—were just the type of maneuvers he'd perfected.

His smile grew.

So, the lovely Jade may have been as affected by him as he had been by her.

The thought gave him such pleasure he was able to walk away without waiting to speak to her. He'd give her some time, but he'd be back.

Jade watched the children leave the lagoon, offering Lae'ula and Polani some fish as a reward for their participation. Adam had disappeared while she'd been distracted, instructing the children in how to signal an aerial leap. But she wasn't sorry to see him go, no matter what her fluttering tummy might be signaling.

It had been a stressful day, what with worrying over

the implications of the previous evening's reception. Thank goodness for the interruption of the swim with the dolphins sessions. Forced to interact with the public, Jade was able to steer her mind away from Adam and her atypical reaction to him.

Finally, Jade sat on the dock at the back of the dolphin pool, gathering her things together. Her first day at work as a marine behaviorist was over.

The sleek gray body of Laka glided past Jade, then doubled back and stopped in front of her. Laka's head came up out of the water and her eyes seemed to look directly into Jade's. Her snout opened in a wide dolphin grin. Jade had to return the smile. She felt sure Laka was trying to tell her that everything would work out. Dolphins had always watched over her and her family. This could be the sign she needed that all would be well.

Jade had always felt a particular connection to sea animals. She was sure it had to do with her Hawaiian heritage and the close interaction of her ancestors with the ocean. She still remembered the day she learned about her family's 'aumakua.

It was the summer after first grade, when she was six. The family was camping at Kawaihae for a week's vacation. Her parents had taught her to always respect the water, and they were very alert about children and water danger.

However, on that day, her parents were busy comforting a hysterical Momi who was only three and had been stung by a bee. They took Momi to the water's edge to rinse the sting, and let the cooling water control the first itch.

It was while there that Jade slipped into the water. She'd always loved the ocean, felt comfortable in it, was never afraid of it. But on that day, Jade overestimated her capacity to swim out to sea. She was far out when she began to tire and turned back toward shore. Too far out. Her little arms and legs were very tired. And the beach was a long way off.

From out of nowhere, a dolphin appeared. The sleek animal swam around her, then moved close enough to allow her to rest against him. He stayed with her until she was able to get ashore on her own. Right into the arms of her frantic parents who had just realized she was missing.

Young as she was, her father told her then about his family's *'aumakua,* the dolphin. Ancient Hawaiians believed that their ancestors watched over them, and their spirits could take the form of earthly things to do so. *'Aumakua* could manifest itself as an animal, plant, or mineral. In this way, the ancestor became easily approachable and could offer guidance and inspiration—and warnings.

In modern times, the old beliefs lived side-by-side with the new. So, although the Kanahele family had long been churchgoing Christians, they still respected the dolphin as their personal *'aumakua.* Family tales abounded of miracles wrought by help from the friendly sea creatures.

Jade determined to work with dolphins as soon as

she was old enough to realize it was a viable career option. And now she was living that dream.

Slinging her backpack over her shoulder, Jade left the lagoon area wearing a wide grin.

Jade didn't see Adam the following day, or the next. She wondered what he was doing. Had he already made a decision about the hotel? Was he even now planning new programs to maximize use of the dolphin lagoon? Would she have the same reaction if he turned up again?

It wasn't until she was packing up her things to leave on Friday afternoon that there was a familiar tickling at the base of her neck. Turning, she saw Adam standing against the wooden railing, watching her solemnly. This awareness she had of his presence was too strange; she wondered if there was any similar connection on his part. Could such strong feelings be one-sided?

The sun cast dark shadows across his face, emphasizing the features that made him so handsome—those high cheekbones and the strong jaw. His neck showed strength as well without being as thick as an elephant's leg. Jade found that especially attractive; she'd never liked the heavy-necked jock look.

"Done for the day?"

Adam's throaty voice floated over the bridge to her, and she resisted an urge to rub her neck where the prickling had intensified. Instead, she shoved a damp T-shirt into her backpack and called out a cheerful reply.

"Yes, I am."

She zipped up the backpack, stood with it in one hand and offered him a dazzling smile. She'd had a rewarding day and was feeling pretty darned good. She loved teaching the children, and she'd had the entire fourth grade from a local school come in that morning. Not just any school, but the elementary school she'd attended. The woman who brought them had been a teacher there when Jade was in attendance; now she was thinking about retirement. But she claimed to remember Jade and spoke highly of her to the children.

And now here was Adam, the man whose presence affected her so intimately. If he wanted to spend some time with her, she might have a chance to educate *him* in the treatment of dolphins. And perhaps learn something of what he meant to do about the Orchid House.

"Are you always so cheerful?"

Adam's voice was grumpy, and Jade's eyes widened as she looked up at him from the lower deck.

"Bad day?"

Adam had been exploring the island, learning about the other hotels and resorts, finding out what was available to tourists. He'd checked the brochures and the Internet, but there was nothing like seeing places for yourself. If they hoped to buy the Orchid House and make it profitable, they had to decide what they could offer that was unique and different.

His travels around the island were not unpleasant. Except for that speeding ticket he'd gotten. The local cops, Adam learned to his chagrin, drove unmarked

54

cars. The only clue to the police vehicles were the small blue lights mounted on the roofs—difficult to see when not flashing.

But driving and examining scenery and local attractions took only a portion of his attention. He'd also spent too much time wishing Jade was in the car with him, giving her opinions of the various places he saw, offering input on his new ideas.

He spent too much time remembering the happiness on her face as he'd seen her tripping along the wooden bridge near the dolphin pool on her way to work. Everyone should be able to head off to work with such delight. He might enjoy scouting out tourist locations, but he certainly wasn't jumping out of bed in the morning, all smiles and sparkling excitement as he suspected she did. He wanted to know her secret.

Instead, he had too much time for introspection. With his thirtieth birthday approaching in just a few days, he was too prone to thinking of his life so far, of what he'd accomplished, and what he hoped to do with it still. And what he'd once hoped to do with it.

Thirty wasn't old, Adam reminded himself yet again. Far from it. Yet at thirty his father had already established himself as a force in the resort industry. And he'd accomplished so much more since then.

Adam tried to think of what he'd accomplished himself. Had any of it been for any good other than the enrichment of the company and hence his father and himself? He'd been an idealistic youth once, planning to do great things for mankind.

But the reality was that few people were able to enrich mankind. The reality was that he worked in the hospitality industry. All he could really hope to do was to make people happy on their vacations. He could create experiences for them to enjoy, allow them to learn about unusual plants and animals, and about other cultures. And that wasn't really so bad, was it?

But a young marine biologist had captured his mind, and suddenly the thing he most wished to accomplish was to spend more time with her.

Yes, he was having a bad day.

He shrugged a wordless reply to her question. He didn't want to go into it.

"If you're on your own time now, would you like to have a drink with me?" He gestured toward the nearby café, the Thatched Hut. "We could sit over there, and you could tell me about your babies."

Adam nodded at the sleek animals swimming in the lagoon, two of whom chose that moment to do a side-by-side leap from the water. A small boy standing beside Adam squealed with delight, clapping his little hands together and jumping up and down.

Adam moved his gaze back to Jade. She was laughing along with the excited little boy. But she'd grinned at his choice of terminology for the dolphins. So he'd chosen correctly; someone who lived such an optimistic life was sure to call the animals her babies.

The thought of Jade and babies threw Adam's thoughts into a whole new direction. What a Madonna she would make, with her lovely oval face and deep, dark eyes. A vision worthy of Boticelli.

Suddenly, Adam didn't want her to think of animals as babies, he wanted her to think about having babies of her own, human babies. His babies.

Sweat broke out on his forehead at the bizarre thought, but it also left an odd feeling in his belly. A hollow spot.

Firmly dismissing any further thoughts of blanket-wrapped bundles held tight against her shapely chest, Adam moved his gaze upward, meeting Jade's eyes. She was still smiling at him.

"I'd like that."

They settled at a table overlooking the dolphin pool. Jade began to tell him about the animals even before their tea arrived. He'd offered something stronger, but she gave a firm shake of her head.

"Iced tea is perfect."

And she continued smiling, while he gave the order to the waitress, while they watched her walk away. Adam noted the way the woman's hips swayed in her brief, tropical-print shorts, but he was a mere observer. The slender waitress did not intrigue him the way Jade did. Jade, the petite marine biologist, who had already started to introduce him to her dolphins.

"I might as well begin with Nahoa, our dominant male. That's him there, showing off." Humor and pride laced her voice as she pointed to the large animal leaping out of the water. "Beautiful, isn't he?"

Adam agreed that he was. And he thought Jade was

57

beautiful too, especially when she spoke of her dolphins. Her face lit with enthusiasm and her hands flew before her in graceful patterns, illustrating her words. She had long, slim fingers, the type usually associated with artists or musicians. They ended with short, practical nails, unpainted, and Adam was amazed at how attractive he found them. In the past, he'd always admired longer nails. Not those super-long nails that looked like an animal's claws, but shapely, well-manicured ones with a natural tint.

Adam pulled his attention from her practical hands, back to her sparkling face, as she continued the introductions.

"Nahoa means 'bold, defiant.' It's a good match to his personality. Trainers usually try to observe the animal for a while before choosing a name. Nahoa is very dominant and likes to be in charge. He's very smart, and is our best aerialist."

As though he could hear her description, Nahoa jumped high out of the water again, higher than before, earning a few audible oohs and ahs from spectators.

Jade indicated another of the sleek mammals, now swimming alongside Nahoa, matching his every leap and dive.

"That's our other male, Polani. His name means handsome, and you can see that he's a very handsome young dolphin. He's quite a bit younger than Nahoa."

Adam lifted one eyebrow. He'd been told he looked like a pirate when he did it, and he wondered what Jade's reaction would be. But he couldn't resist teasing her a little about the definitive statement she had just made.

"How do you know how old they are?"

Pirate or not, Jade was not intimidated.

"Ve haf our methods," she told him in her best imitation of an early talkies melodrama villain. One of her eyebrows quirked upward as she finished. She was matching him move for move.

Adam laughed. "Seriously."

"Ahh, seriously."

Jade assumed the expression he'd seen her wear as she lectured the children and tourists at the lagoon.

"Worn down teeth can be one sign. Maturation rates. And it helps date a female if she has a baby. Female dolphins generally give birth to their first baby at around twelve to fifteen years of age."

"So it's an imprecise science." He nodded, more to himself than to Jade. It made more sense that the numbers were guesstimates.

Jade didn't dispute him.

"Male dolphins are very social and set up friendships with other males that seem to last throughout their lifetime. Polani and Nahoa have that kind of relationship here in our little pod."

Their waitress arrived with their tea, and Jade remained silent during the time it took to lay down coasters and place the glasses on them. Once the waitress was gone, Jade took a long sip then resumed her discourse.

"Polani loves to play and can be quite mischievous."

Adam added sweetner to his tea and stirred it. "Sounds like a small child."

Jade laughed. "More like a teenager. He's just maturing, so he probably acts like a teenager. We took him in when he was caught in some fishing nets. He almost died, but he'd doing very well here now."

"So he was a rescue project."

Jade nodded, sipping her tea. "Operations like ours often receive animals that way."

Adam nodded absently, his eyes serious as he took in the lagoon and the milling animals. The lagoon was a big plus on the credit side of the hotel's score sheet. But how big?

"The dolphin there with the little one swimming beside her is Laka with her son Kei. It was the first birth here at Dolphin Life Research, and we're very proud of how healthy Kei has been. And, in case you're wondering, Nahoa is his father."

Jade watched the animals swim for a moment, a soft smile tilting her lips. "Laka means 'gentle,' and she has a very gentle and charming personality. She would make a wonderful therapy dolphin."

"Therapy dolphin?" He didn't pretend not to know what that meant.

"I'm not endorsing therapy dolphins. It's a very specialized field. I'm just saying that Laka's personality would be good for that kind of work."

Jade hesitated, as though waiting for Adam to say more. When he didn't, she took a sip of her tea and continued.

"Kei means 'one's pride and joy.' There was a contest to name the dolphin baby and school children from all over the island sent in suggestions. Kei was the name chosen by a panel of judges that included the mayor and a state representative. Kei is full of energy and is very curious, especially about people."

Adam watched as Jade examined the dolphin lagoon. He knew there were five dolphins, counting the baby, Kei. The resort played up the presence of the dolphins as much as they did the atrium orchid greenhouse, from which the resort took its name. Adam didn't know yet how many of the guests took the tour of the greenhouse, but he felt sure every one of them walked past the dolphin pool at least once during their stay. Maybe even once a day. There always seemed to be a crowd standing along the railings that bordered the dolphin lagoon. And hundreds of guests entered the swim with the dolphins lotteries daily.

Adam turned his attention back to Jade as she described the last of the dolphins.

"The final member of our pod is Lae'ula. Her name means 'well-trained, clever,' and she is that." Jade pointed to a dolphin "standing" on her tail near the bridge that crossed over the lagoon, scooting backward through the water. Visitors stood shoulder to shoulder on the bridge, exclaiming over her. "Lae'ula was born in captivity, though not here of course. She's always the first to learn new tricks and games, and she can be a real show-off." She gestured toward the lagoon. "She loves to perform for the crowd and can be very charismatic."

Adam nodded as she finished her description of the final member of the pod. A smile nudged at the corner of his mouth. He could watch her talk about the dolphins all day.

Then she met his eyes, flashing him an answering grin. Excitement flared in her dark eyes.

"This isn't general knowledge yet," she told him, dropping her voice before she shared her secret, "but Lae'ula is pregnant. I'm telling you because I know you're in negotiations to purchase the hotel, so you have the right to know. Baby dolphins are a big attraction. But I would appreciate it if you wouldn't let everyone know."

He met her eyes, a pleasant feeling of warmth spreading through him at her trust. "Certainly."

Chapter Four

For a moment, they drank their iced tea in silence, nibbling on potato skins and watching the dolphins swim and leap. Adam asked her again to join him for dinner, but Jade declined. Claiming hunger and the length of time since lunch, he'd insisted on ordering an appetizer. He felt grateful to have something to do with his hands. He was feeling a powerful urge to reach over and touch her. He still remembered the warm softness of her skin from their brief contact earlier in the week. Would her skin feel the same—smooth and warm? Or would it be dry and sticky after a day in the saltwater lagoon? Would she mind if he tucked that strand of hair back into place? It drifted across her cheek as tempting as a cold drink on a hot summer's day.

Attempting to put such images from his mind, Adam turned his attention back to the dolphins.

"They're large."

Jade laughed at his wry understatement, a wonderful musical sound that was pleasant on the ear. Still, one side of his mouth drew downward as he examined her. She was all woman, with an athletic body. But she was petite. He didn't like to think of her in that lagoon with such enormous animals. *Wild* animals, for all their training and tricks.

"The females are about seven feet long and weigh from four hundred to four hundred and fifty pounds. The males are a bit larger."

"Just a bit?"

"Um-hmm."

She refused to give in to his new mood. She continued to smile, teasing.

"The males are eight to nine feet long. Polani weighs just over five hundred pounds, and Nahoa almost six hundred."

Adam frowned at her. Didn't she see any danger here?

"And how much do you weigh? About a hundred pounds soaking wet?"

"Why, Adam Donovan, you should know that a lady never reveals her weight." Amusement rippled through the words.

But Adam wasn't ready to joke about it.

"I'm thinking of you in the water with those giant animals every day. Isn't it dangerous? One flip of the tail and you could be history."

Jade shook her head. "Don't be silly. I'm a trained marine behaviorist. I know what I'm doing, and how to act in the water with the animals."

She started to reach for a potato skin, but changed her mind. Instead she used her hand to emphasize what she had to say.

"But that is an inherent problem with the swim with the dolphin programs. Some hotels want to let anyone swim in the dolphin pool, as long as they can afford to pay for the privilege. They don't realize that those sweet looking animals with their wide grins aren't all friendly like Flipper. They're big and they can be dangerous. The same with the humpback whales. Boats take tourists out to see the whales in the wintertime and people want to get out and swim with them. It's foolish behavior at best and stupid and deadly at worst. A woman died this past winter when she was pulled underwater by a whale she was petting." Jade could barely control herself, her hand swinging upward as she expressed her frustration. "Petting it! I mean, really! Did she think it was a dog? Wild animals should be allowed to be wild animals."

Adam stared. Jade could certainly become passionate over her animals. And what that fervor did for her appearance! Her eyes sparkled with enthusiasm, flashing with zeal as she spoke. Her cheeks were flushed with color, her hands moving with graceful abandon as she used them to emphasize her points.

"So you don't approve of swim with the dolphin programs then?"

Adam asked the question with a straight face, his voice conversational but as serious as he could make it. He almost spoiled it by laughing when Jade stared at him, her eyes wide with what he thought might be outrage. Or maybe disgust.

Then she looked closer and her facial features softened. One side of her mouth twitched.

"What was your first clue?" she asked.

He had to laugh then too.

"But seriously, Adam, dolphins living in captivity have stress-related conditions. We're quite proud of the fact that none of our dolphins suffer from ulcers. Ulcers are very common among captive dolphins. Too much human interaction can worsen problems like that, and can also cause behavior problems. In some foreign countries where there is little supervision of dolphin conditions, captive dolphins have exhibited agitated and aggressive behavior toward humans. Some serious injuries have been reported."

"Such as . . . ?"

"Lacerations, tooth rakes, broken bones."

Their waitress came by with a pitcher and refilled their glasses. Adam emptied a packet of sweetner into his glass, his expression thoughtful as he stirred. "I can see there's a lot more to this than digging a lagoon and hiring a trainer."

"A lot more."

Adam thought she looked like she wanted to say more, but she picked up her glass instead. He pursed his lips as he watched her. She was smart. Giving him time to think over all the information she'd provided was the intelligent thing to do. Harping too long on the subject could make a person resent both the speaker and the cause.

Was she attempting to manipulate him? He almost smiled at the thought. He'd fought antagonists much more difficult than Jade. She didn't seem the manipulative type. But then he should have learned by now that those types rarely did.

"So, have you ever gone swimming with dolphins yourself? Besides here in the lagoon, I mean."

"Of course I've gone swimming with dolphins." Jade raised her chin to a defiant angle. "I'm a trained dolphin behaviorist. I've participated in studies that included swimming with dolphins in the wild."

She met his steady gaze across the table, determined not to change her position on an issue she felt so strongly about. Whether or not she might be using him, Adam had to admire her. She was fighting for what she believed in. In her view, he was the enemy.

He continued to stir his tea. "So, what is it like?"

"Well, for those who know what they're doing," she began, emphasizing the words, "it can be the most incredible experience." Her eyes took on a faraway look. "There's something mystical about dolphins, about interacting with them out there in their world."

Her head turned so that she looked out over the ocean. Adam's gaze followed hers. The sun was setting, dropping down toward the ocean in the rapid manner of a tropical sunset. The sky was beautiful, pink and peach and a little purple, with the remaining portion of the sun's orb a deep orange. Far out to sea, in a direct line between their table and the descending sun, Adam was amazed to see what had to be a pod of dolphins leaping out of the water. He saw Jade smile. She didn't seem surprised to see them.

"The dolphin is my family's *'aumakua*. To put it simply, that's like a special ancestral spirit who takes the form of a dolphin and watches out for us. So I have a personal connection to them. But that first time I swam out in Kealakekua Bay with the wild spinner dolphins, it was magical."

Her eyes remained on his face, but he knew she wasn't seeing him. Her inner vision was far south beyond the coastline of resorts, down in Kealakekua Bay.

"You can feel them before you see them, because of their echolocation—the sonar. You hear a buzzing in the water, and then feel an odd tingling sensation. It seems to enter your body and set all your organs vibrating."

She grinned at him, her eyes once more focused on the scene in front of her.

"The echolocation clicks transmit through water, you know, and human bodies are largely composed of water. So that buzzing vibration goes through your body, just as it travels through the ocean water. It's very strange the first time you feel it."

"But not bad, I take it."

"Oh, no." Her response was rapid. "The peace and serenity you feel, being out there among them . . . it's almost impossible to describe."

Adam's laugh was wry.

"I could use a little peace and serenity in my life."

Jade's eyebrows rose. "Having a midlife crisis, are we?"

"Midlife?" Adam laughed, but the sound was less than pleasant. "Hardly."

Jade laughed this time, a much more agreeable sound.

"Do you like to hike?"

If Jade was surprised by the abrupt change in subject, she didn't show it. She merely answered the question, her cheerful expression once more in place.

"I love to hike. I don't often have the opportunity. Mostly I swim for exercise. Why?"

"I noticed some hiking trails on the hotel map, over on the other side of the golf course."

"Oh, yes. There's a good trail carved out of the lava fields, and a huge petroglyph field."

"I guess you're familiar with it then. With the inactivity, and the rich food, I'm feeling badly out of shape. I was thinking of going hiking tomorrow. I think you said it was your day off?"

Jade arched one brow. Adam? Out of shape? Never had she seen anyone in better shape. The man was beautiful.

"Are you asking me to go with you?"

The right side of his mouth quirked upward into that wry smile of his. Darn but he looked good when he did that.

"I guess I'm not doing a very good job. Would you like to come with me? Be my guide?"

Still focused on his mouth, Jade almost missed the question. The way her heart beat whenever he looked at her, it might be best to avoid being too much in his company. On the other hand, she liked being with him, enjoyed that surge of life that pulsed through her veins when he was near. And she'd enjoy the hike too. Besides, it would be another opportunity to get close to him. Eventually, he might drop his guard and actually tell her something.

"I'd love to go. I haven't done those trails for years."

"Is it good hiking?"

"Yes, it is, a good aerobic workout. And I'd love to see the petroglyphs again. I understand the hotel has taken some measures to protect them, putting up fences and viewing platforms."

She thought for a moment. "There are the remains of an old *heiau,* too." She looked at Adam. "That's an old temple area."

He nodded and she went on.

"It's at the end of the trail area, overlooking the sea. There's a small bay there and sometimes the dolphins come in close to shore. Some of us kayak out there and swim with them."

"Sounds like you'll make an excellent guide."

She shrugged but the comment pleased her.

Adam smiled. He did have a wonderful smile. It made his eyes sparkle with fun, causing little wrinkles to appear near them that gave his face character. And she didn't even want to think about what happened to her heart rate when she noticed the way one side of his mouth quirked upward more than the other.

"Is it a good place for snorkeling?" he asked.

"It is. Do you snorkel, then?"

"I do. Could we go into the bay from the trail, if we bring equipment with us?"

"No. There's a long drop from the end of the trail, and the beach isn't friendly. You have to approach from the ocean."

Her hand moved out in a graceful wave that encompassed a wide area beyond the dolphin lagoon. A series of long, low buildings faced the water, housing groups that offered everything from glass-bottomed boat tours to parasailing adventures. The people working in those buildings during the day were the same ones who had been at the reception on Monday night.

"Out on the beachfront here, you can sign up for a snorkeling trip on an outrigger canoe. My cousin runs Sea Explorations, and sometimes I help out by guiding a group. It's a lot of fun, especially with the teens."

Adam's exploration of the island began to take on an element of excitement. Perhaps he needed her cheerful optimism to enable him to see what special options were available.

Her description of swimming with wild dolphins sounded like so much new age gibberish to him. Yet there was no question of the effect it had on her. Even just talking about it, her face had taken on an expression of serene peace that he coveted. He wanted to spend more time with her, to explore the chemistry between them. Perhaps some of her tranquility would rub off on him too.

Jade was reading in bed that evening when the telephone rang. Wondering who might be calling so late, she was pleased to hear her sister's voice greet her.

"Momi! How are you? All settled in?"

Momi, at twenty-one, just three years younger than Jade, had returned to Honolulu for a summer job as a library intern.

"Oh, yeah. My roommate had everything all set up; all I had to do was unpack my clothes. But I want to hear about the new job and that reception you were so anxious to attend."

Her teasing voice almost made Jade wince. She still remembered the teasing she'd endured from her sisters at dinner the previous weekend. Ruby, their youngest sister, had been especially annoying, telling Jade she'd be sure to meet a rich *haole* at the resort. And where better to start than at a fancy evening reception?

As if she'd even want to meet a rich *haole* after her experience with Teddy. But then that's what having sisters was all about.

"I love the job, but you already know that."

"Yep. So tell me about the party."

"It was great. You should have seen the food!"

"The food? I call long distance from Honolulu and all you can talk about is the food?"

Jade could tease too. "You don't like food?"

Momi laughed. "Okay. Do it your way. Just tell me all about it."

So Jade described the people in attendance and the delicious food. "You've seen the hotel, so you know the room was beautiful. I wanted to stare at everything like the country hick I am."

"Pooh. You're no country hick. You've been all over the world."

"Just to research dolphins."

"You must have seen some of the sights while you were traveling. You went snorkeling at the Great Barrier Reef."

Jade had to admit that that was true. It was a fabulous experience too, one she would always treasure.

"And you've seen a lot of islands in the Caribbean."

This time Jade laughed. "I was mostly collecting data for a dolphin study then. I had to pretend to be a tourist. I saw a lot of water parks."

"Still, you've been all over." Momi heaved a giant sigh. "I've never even been out of the state."

Jade laughed. "Don't forget half the residents of the mainland would kill to see this state."

Momi giggled. "I guess we lucky we born Hawaii."

Jade laughed too at the popular local saying.

But she sobered quickly as she thought of the resort and all the people who might be anxious to vacation there—especially if they could be assured of a chance to swim with the dolphins.

"The guest of honor was an Adam Donovan."

When she didn't continue, Momi's voice came back at her.

"And . . . ?"

"The rumor is that he's looking into buying the hotel for his family's company."

She heard Momi's sharp intake of breath. "So it's true what you heard. They are selling."

"Well, it hasn't come from official sources, but there are too many rumors for it to be unfounded."

"Did you meet him?"

"Um-hmm."

There was a moment of silence.

"Well?"

"Well, what?" Jade asked.

"Well, what was he like?" Momi's voice almost exploded down the line. Jade would have laughed at the memories it brought of their childhood years if she hadn't been so involved in thinking about Adam. Jade wanted to tell Momi about him, but where to start? What to say? She couldn't very well tell her younger sister about the strange sensations she felt deep inside whenever he was near. Of the warmth that flooded her at his touch of her hand.

"It's hard to say," Jade finally said. "He doesn't let anyone really get to know him. He's devastatingly handsome. Tall, dark blue eyes that really look at you. He wore a suit to the reception."

"Really?"

"Yeah. That's how you could tell it was business."

"I guess." Not many islanders dressed so formally.

"But tell me more about how he looked."

Jade could hear the teasing smile in her sister's voice.

"Oh, just real good-looking," she said. "But kind of arrogant too, you know? Like he could squash you like a bug if he really wanted to."

"Yikes. And you liked this guy?"

"I don't know," Jade admitted. "There's something about him." She wouldn't tell Momi that the something had to do with physical chemistry. "And he doesn't look at *me* that way. We talked about the work at Dolphin Life. I wanted to get in as much lobbying as I could."

"I'll bet." Then Momi laughed. "So you have met Ruby's rich *haole*. Think there's any romance there?"

Jade hesitated until Momi spoke again.

"Sounds like there's a possibility."

This brought a rapid response from Jade. "What do you mean 'a possibility'? There's no romance. I just met him."

"Yeah, yeah."

Jade frowned at the red and white quilt folded down at the bottom of her bed.

"Momi, the strangest thing happened this weekend. You know when I was at the house to see if there was anything else in my old room that I would need?"

"Uh-huh. You came in just as Ruby and I left for Grandma Lucas' to say good-bye." Their sister Ruby had just graduated from high school and was going to spend the summer in Hilo staying with a cousin while she worked a summer job. They'd had a big family dinner together last Sunday, just the five of them, before the girls all scattered for the summer.

"Yeah. Well, while I was there, Mom gave me a quilt."

"Really? Another one? Gee, do you think I'll get another one when I finish graduate school? Is it from Grandma Lucas? What's the pattern?"

Jade pulled air into her lungs, breathless at Momi's torrent of questions.

"It's not from Grandma Lucas. This is a really old quilt. You should see it. It's beautiful, red and white, though the white is so old it's yellowing. There are all kinds of flowers and leaves on it, making the prettiest pattern." Jade leaned over, stroking Hina's furry head, but peering at the folded quilt at the foot of the bed as she spoke. "Mom called it *Ka Makani Ka'ili Aloha,* which means the wind that wafts love from one to another."

She heard Momi draw in a breath.

"That's beautiful. It must be wonderful. How come I've never seen it? And why'd Mom give it to you now?"

Jade knew that Momi was not asking out of envy. Simple curiosity prompted the question.

"That's the really strange part. Mom called it the Lovell women's legacy."

"Legacy?"

"Sounds like a bad movie, doesn't it?"

Momi agreed.

"See, the thing is, this quilt is supposed to be some kind of a love potion."

"What?"

Jade could hear the incredulity in her sister's voice. But at least she wasn't laughing herself silly.

"It's so ridiculous, I can't believe I'm telling you about it."

"Well, if it's the Lovell family legacy, then it's my legacy too."

This time Jade heard amusement in her sister's voice. But it was quickly replaced with a serious curiosity.

"So how does it work?"

"Mom didn't really say. Only that within days of getting the quilt, she, her mother, and her grandmother all met the men of their dreams. And they were all married within a year of receiving the quilt. So it works quickly."

"How did she explain the love potion bit?"

"It had to do with the great love Helen Lovell Keahi had for her husband and unborn child, the love that she poured into the quilt as she worked on it."

"The *mana*."

"Exactly."

Momi was silent for a moment and Jade could picture her, brows drawn together, forehead furrowed in concentration. She was probably sitting on the bed, too, just as Jade was.

"That must be what Mom and Dad were talking about after you left that night. Something about a quilt and whether the reception would do the trick. And whether the manager might be the one. Remember, you said the resort manager had invited you to a reception. Ruby and I thought it was all pretty strange."

"What?" Jade almost shouted the word, startling poor Hina who flipped over, capturing Jade's hand in her paws. The cat bit Jade's thumb and scraped her palm with her claws. "They think I'm dating the resort manager? He's married!"

"I'm sure they don't know that," Momi pointed out. Then her voice quieted, becoming almost solemn, and definitely hesitant. "Do you think it will work?"

"Momi!" Jade could not believe that Momi would ask such a question in a serious manner. How could she? They were modern women of the twenty-first century. They didn't believe in love potions.

Momi laughed, her voice teasing. "Well, you did meet that 'devastatingly handsome' guy at the reception. Adam of the dark blue eyes."

"He's just here temporarily—on business. And *his* business might be very bad for mine," Jade added.

"He's still a man." Momi's voice was teasing once more.

The words stirred a memory in Jade—of similar words carried on the ocean breeze.

The remembered words, soft as a whisper, caused a shiver to snake up Jade's spine. Her eyes flew to the antique quilt.

"Yeah, he must be my true love."

But the words weren't the sarcastic denial she'd meant to utter.

Jade frowned. She didn't believe in love potion mumbo jumbo.

"Honestly, Momi, we just met."

But her sister wasn't ready to let it go.

"Have you seen him again?"

"Of course. He's around the hotel a lot."

Momi's voice was thoughtful. "Why do I get the feeling you're not telling me everything here?"

"Well, we are going hiking tomorrow," Jade admitted. "But he just asked me because I'm familiar with the trail and he wanted a guide."

Momi laughed. "Sure."

"Listen, I've got to get going. Another work day tomorrow morning."

"It's tough going back after a break." Momi sighed. "Are you still in alt about starting your job at the resort?"

"Of course. How could you even ask? Don't you like your job?"

Momi had had a variety of jobs throughout her college years, her latest as an intern at a library in Honolulu.

"Sure. I especially like this one, actually. But sometimes I just feel like I'd rather sleep in. Especially on a Saturday."

It was Jade's turn to laugh. It was great talking to Momi.

After their good-byes, she dropped her book to the floor beside the bed, then reached over to rub Hina's head. Her palm stung from the scratch she'd gotten earlier. Luckily it hadn't bled all over the bedsheets.

"You should be ashamed of yourself, scratching me that way," she scolded gently.

The cat's purr rumbled loudly as she looked at Jade through slitted eyes.

"I'll take that as an apology. I know I scared you, didn't I?"

With a final pat to the tabby's head, Jade turned off the light and settled into the pillows.

Chapter Five

Early the next morning, Adam stood at the trailhead awaiting Jade, his anticipation of her presence beyond anything he'd expected to feel. The stark lava fields stretched out beyond him, black rock as far as the eye could see. The sight of these acres of desolation gave him a better appreciation of what must have been involved in building the Orchid House Resort. Ten years ago, there was no resort, no lush gardens, no dolphin pool—just more lava reaching all the way to the ocean. To see the resort today, green and lush with tropical plantings, it seemed an incredible feat.

And yet even that did not move him as much as the sight of Jade's compact body striding toward him. Her hair was neatly plaited, the way she wore it for working in the dolphin pool. He was unable to see her face as yet, just the outline of her lithe body and the halo of wispy curls that refused to be tamed framing her face. Although she was not tall, her female form was well defined; curves in all the right places, a nipped-in waist, legs long in proportion to her body, their length shown off to advantage in khaki shorts.

Her body language proclaimed her awake and ready. She strode toward him with a bounce to her step that relayed her optimistic view of the world. He knew there would be a big smile on her lips, and a sparkle in her eye, which was confirmed when she stood before him.

"Aloha. I hope I didn't keep you waiting."

The cheerful tone of her voice reinforced his original impression of her attitude. And it did seem to be rubbing off on him. He felt darn good this morning.

"Not at all." Adam had no intention of admitting that he'd been ready for an hour, at the trailhead itself for fifteen minutes. Normally impatient if forced to wait, he'd appeared early in some irrational hope that his presence would induce hers. Seeing her now kicked his heartbeat into high gear. He wanted to reach out and undo her careful braid, run his fingers through her dark mass of curls.

Adam curbed his fantasies, holding up his backpack. "I brought along water and sunscreen. And an extra hat," he added, eyeing her bare head.

"I have one," she answered, pulling a fabric hat

from her pocket. She unfolded the white fabric, tugging it back into its proper shape. "But I'm glad to hear you're well prepared. I brought water and sunscreen too." She adjusted a wide belt equipped with a water bottle and fanny pack. "A lot of tourists don't take into consideration how intense the sun is here."

"Ah, but I've been living in the tropics," he told her.

"Really? You didn't say much about yourself the other day. And last night all we talked about were my dolphins."

She grinned. He hoped that meant it was a pleasant memory.

"So where do you live?" Jade asked.

"I grew up in Florida, but in recent years I've lived all over. Lately, I've been working in Mexico."

Adam bowed his head as he indicated the start of the trail. "Shall we begin?"

Jade immediately set the hat on her head, adjusted the brim to the proper angle and strode forward. Adam hastened to join her.

Jade was a small woman. The top of her head barely hit his chin. Or would if she were snuggled up against him. A distracting image of the two of them on a dance floor appeared, her head resting against his chest, her eyes closed, her hair tickling the underside of his jaw.

It took a brief shake of the head to return himself to the present.

The trail began simply enough, a well-defined path carved through extensive fields of black lava. Numerous signs warned hikers not to stray, of danger beyond the marked trail. But as they walked, Adam realized they were moving uphill. The grade was small, but he could feel it in his calf muscles. It had been much too long since he'd done a real workout. Too many meetings; too much number crunching.

A quick glance at Jade told him she was in top condition. She continued to move forward at the same stride, her breathing even, with no noticeable strain.

It was a beautiful sunny morning, the temperature comfortable, the wind a mere breeze. But the direct sun falling on their shoulders, the high humidity, and the exercise itself soon had sweat rolling off their bodies.

As they paused for a drink, Adam watched a bead of moisture roll down Jade's face, along the smooth skin just in front of her ear. Giving in to temptation, he reached out and caught it on his fingertip. Her skin was soft, smooth as satin, and so warm. Heat seared his finger and worked its way up his arm and into his chest, fanning out into his body.

Adam gulped his water, discovering a sudden and overwhelming need for the cooling liquid. As he replaced the bottle, his eyes locked on hers. So dark he could hardly distinguish between iris and pupil, he was held by a fleeting look of astonishment that passed over her. Then she blinked, stepped back, and pulled out a handkerchief to wipe her face. Not a tiny scrap of linen with embroidered flowers and a lace border. Jade's hanky was a large cotton square—a practical and functional accessory.

"Ladies aren't supposed to sweat, we're supposed to glow," Jade said with a chuckle that even to her own ears sounded forced. "I don't know though, I must be glowing enough to light up the island."

She returned her water and hanky to their proper places and prepared to resume their hike.

She was almost afraid to meet Adam's eyes. Her reaction to this man had been completely unexplainable right from the first.

She'd rushed up the trail hoping to get started before he noticed how her eyes wanted to devour his athletic figure. Even wearing the baggy shorts that were the current fashion, it was obvious what a gorgeous hunk of man he was. Hard to believe he'd wanted to hike because he felt out of shape. He looked like he worked out regularly, or played some kind of sport. Not golf, something active like tennis or basketball. Muscle defined and shaped his arms and legs, probably his chest, too, though that was covered by his shirt and out of her view. And something that took him outdoors, because he had a great tan.

Wanting to distract herself from his good looks she'd rushed up the trail, barely speaking to him. And she would have liked to hear more about his life in Mexico, too, or his childhood in Florida. Instead, she'd practically run for her life. What must he think of her?

Heat flooded her body as she thought about how he'd touched her face just now! If her face wasn't already flushed from the exercise, she was sure she would have become as red and hot as an electric burner. His finger seared a path down her skin. She'd wanted to turn her face into his touch, rest her cheek against his palm.

Goodness, Jade thought. *I'm beginning to act like Hina! Next I'll be purring!*

Disgusted with the direction of her thoughts, Jade turned toward Adam—with a smile, of course.

"Come on, slow poke."

"Hey, I can take you easily."

Her smile widened. "Is that a challenge?"

Adam grinned, his blue eyes twinkling with merriment. "Let's go."

They walked quickly, Jade enjoying the challenge of keeping up with the larger man.

After five minutes with neither of them attaining a noticeable lead, Jade spoke.

"We're approaching the petroglyph field."

Jade was proud of the strong quality of her voice. At this pace, in another minute or two she would have been struggling to speak and walk at the same time. But her words slowed Adam, and once again she matched his pace.

She gestured toward a boardwalk visible up ahead, an incongruous sight in the black lava field. Jade explained that it had been added two years before in an attempt to preserve the petroglyph field.

"People were actually trying to remove bits of rock, so they could take a symbol home with them for a souvenir." Her voice expressed her horror.

But Adam understood. "It's incredible what some people will do. But that's a problem shared by all ancient sites. I've been working in Mexico for the past year, and it's an enormous problem there too. There, it's often the local people who vandalize sites. There's so much poverty and the local peasants can't understand why they shouldn't take and sell old objects they find in the area. They've been doing it for hundreds of years."

The brief conversation brought them to the viewing platform, where Jade and Adam decided on some rest time. They leaned against the wooden rail, sipping from water bottles, and examined the ancient carvings.

"No one really knows what the petroglyphs mean," Jade told him. "Some of them go pretty far back in time. Modern scholars interpret the symbols in certain ways, but no one can be sure if their interpretation is correct."

Adam grinned. "I think I see the symbol for man."

Jade could feel the heat flood her face, and not from the sun or the temperatures.

"Just like a man. They're all absorbed by their interest in just one thing."

"Oh, there might be another . . ."

"Some of the drawings are fairly obvious." Jade cut him off, her cheeks still burning. The wind had picked up and she welcomed the cool breeze on her face. "Like that *paniolo*," she added, pointing to what had to be a man on a horse. She stepped to the side, away from Adam and indicated another carving. "Or that turtle."

"This one looks like two men boxing," Adam told her, bringing her attention to two stick figures with upraised fists.

For at least fifteen minutes they poured over the primitive carvings, pointing out interesting figures to each other. It was when a large group of tourists appeared, many of them gasping for breath after the long walk to the site, that Adam and Jade decided to continue on the trail. After passing through the petroglyph field, it headed toward the ocean. The lava trail resumed just beyond the viewing platforms built to protect the petroglyphs, and moved slowly downhill.

After another half hour of brisk walking, they stood on a rocky cliff overlooking the ocean. The drop wasn't too great, but still some ten to twelve feet down to where the waves crashed against a rock-strewn shore. The wind was stronger here and heavy with salt spray. While it cooled their bodies, it created other problems. Adam just saved his hat, catching it after it blew off his head, headed for the ocean beyond. Jade removed hers as a precautionary measure, folding it and slipping it back into her pocket.

Jade pointed out the area where she and her friends sometimes went snorkeling.

"It's a good area. There's a coral reef there, and we see a lot of sea turtles in addition to the usual fish."

They stood on the promontory for some time, admiring the view, while the wind whipped around them. Jade pointed out the rocks that she claimed were the remains of an ancient *heiau,* or temple. Adam thought they looked much like all the rest of the black rock in the area. But closer examination showed these had been carefully placed, forming a flattened platform.

There was no question that the area was beautiful. Raw and natural, it would be a shame to ruin it with another carefully tended expanse of golf course fairways. Behind them the mountain was green with pastures and dotted with moving dark spots that must be cattle. Clouds shrouded the topmost section of the mountain. The blue ocean stretched out for thousands of miles.

"It's wonderful, isn't it?" Jade flung her arms wide and turned until she'd made a full circle. Her face shone, not only from perspiration and salt spray, but from joy at the beautiful landscape laid out before them.

"It certainly is." Adam's voice was thick. She looked terrific. Vibrant, vital—Adam couldn't come up with enough adjectives to describe the life that emanated from her compact body. Hair had escaped from her careful braid, fluffing out around her head like an angel's halo.

She pointed across the water at a strange looking cloud. Adam thought it had the appearance of a dream castle, then instantly dismissed the fanciful thought.

"You can see Maui today."

"That hazy cloud is Maui?" Adam looked again. Not a dream castle. A dream island.

Jade laughed, a wonderful sound that wound up Adam's spine and tickled him into an answering smile.

"It's Haleakala, the largest mountain on Maui."

"I've heard of it."

His wry voice sent her off into further gales of laughter. What a wonderful, musical sound came from those lips. Adam's eyes focused on them—those full lips, a bit too wide, yet so very appealing. And such a delicious shade of pink. Would they taste of salt from the sea air and her recent exercise?

The thought of a kiss drained all other thoughts from his mind. The ocean, the mountain, the beautiful landscape, faded from his vision. All he could see was her face, her lips. All he could think of was the magic of touching his lips to hers.

Adam had never met anyone who so enjoyed life. Jade reveled in simple everyday experiences—in going to work, in exercise, in the sight of the everyday landscape. It gave him a whole new perspective.

He was still staring at her, dreaming of the moment when their lips would meet, when she turned and saw him.

"What?"

The question was followed by a quick glance down at herself.

"Do I have dirt on my face? On my shirt?"

Adam just shook his head. He knew it was rude to stare, but it was very hard to resist when standing next to someone as compelling as Jade. The thought of a kiss was irresistible. Adam stepped closer, lowering his head.

Jade's eyes widened as he moved closer. Adam hesitated, just long enough to halt if she indicated a reluctance to participate. Thankfully, she did not object.

His lips touched hers. Their bodies were close but did not meet, heat from their recent exercise radiating outward, filling the space between them. The kiss was light, ephemeral. A fleeting taste of honey. It was all he wanted for now. All he needed.

Their acquaintance was brief, as transient as his kiss, but as exciting as the brush of her lips on his.

Her lips were just as he'd imagined. Warm and smooth, they tasted of the sea. A totally appropriate taste for Jade. There was no separating her from the sea.

The moment was short-lived, but Adam found it immensely satisfying.

As his lips left hers, he stepped back, keeping his eyes on Jade's face. Would she be angry?

Jade stared back at him, her eyes moving quickly from his lips to his eyes, and back again. Then she reached for her water, but held the bottle in her hand without lifting it. Adam felt a flash of pride; she didn't want to wash his taste away.

The special moment was broken by the loud roar of a helicopter flying overhead. Adam shot a disgusted look upward before fixing his gaze back on Jade. Unable to resist, he reached forward, touching his fingers to her cheek. He trailed it lightly down to her chin.

"You fascinate me."

Her eyebrows flew upward in genuine surprise. The corners of his mouth twitched with a hard-to-ignore impulse to grin.

"You do. You're so happy all the time. I've seen you going in to work in the morning, and I can see the happiness flowing off you. It's unreal."

Now Jade was staring at him. Was his reaction so strange?

"Even now. You know how to enjoy life. Look at the pleasure you find looking out over the landscape." He shook his head. "I think it's beautiful here, and it certainly is nice to see it. But I don't find that joy in it that you do. That has to be a gift, Jade. I wish you could share it with me."

Jade continued to view Adam in amazement.

"Are so many people you know unhappy that you think my attitude is so strange?"

Adam didn't care for her choice of words.

"Not strange. Just unusual. And it's just an impression, not a comment on my acquaintances."

Jade glanced out at the landscape around them. "I don't think I'm so unusual. I appreciate nature and the environment, and I feel lucky to work outdoors and with animals I love."

Adam nodded. He'd known that about her; it was obvious.

"I love working with kids too. That's another part of my job that I love. The animals are wonderful, and I feel privileged to work with them. But I love that I can share my knowledge with so many children. I hope that I can teach them about dolphins so that they'll appreciate them too and work to save them."

The water bottle was still in her hand, and she lifted it to her mouth for a long drink.

"Maybe it's the nature of your job then." Adam's smile was wry. "You have such lofty ideals. It's not quite on the same scale as operating resort hotels. And high-end ones at that."

But she came quickly to his defense.

"There's a lot to be said for operating resorts. You provide people with a pleasant place to get away, to relax and recoup. That's important too, just in a different way. It's good for people's health, both mental and physical, to have that time away to relax."

Adam shook his head again. "You're amazing. Can you find something good about everything?"

Jade scrunched up her nose. "You make me sound like a real Pollyanna." She frowned. "I don't think I'm like that at all."

"People rarely see themselves as others do," Adam told her.

He rubbed a finger lightly over her frown. "Don't do that. You'll get wrinkles before your time."

Her cheeks were pink from the recent exercise, her lips an enticing shade of rose. He saw her as a lovely, beautiful woman, a woman who made his hormones race. That brief kiss had singed his soul.

Frightened at the intensity of his response, Adam pulled his hand back, and took a last look around.

"Shall we start back or do you want to sit and rest awhile?"

"What? After all the rest we've already had? You think I'm a wimp?" Bright, dark eyes turned toward him, laughing, full of mischief. "Of course if *you* want to rest . . ."

Adam found himself laughing in response to her challenge.

"Hey, I'm going to be thirty next week. I have to take it a little easier than you twenty-year-old kids."

"I don't believe it." Jade laughed. "So that's what the midlife crisis is all about."

"It's not a midlife crisis. I'm too young for that."

She was still laughing.

"So what is it? Fear?" Jade's eyebrow arched upward. "Don't tell me a big brave fellow like you is scared of hitting thirty? I thought that went out in the seventies."

"I'm not frightened." His voice was hard. He started back up the trail and Jade fell in beside him. "Birthdays that end in zero are landmarks, that's all. It just has me thinking."

"What about?"

They walked slower now, much of their energy concentrated on their words.

"Life. Nostalgia, maybe. I've been thinking about my childhood. About my mother, who died just as I finished high school."

Jade's eyes instantly clouded. "I'm so sorry."

Adam shrugged. "It's a long time ago now. But at

the time it was . . ." he paused, thinking of the proper word, ". . . difficult," he finally said.

Jade didn't say anything to that, and he was grateful. There were some things that required no response. And he hated pity.

He continued moving forward, concentrating on placing one foot in front of the other.

"Remember those 'what I want to be when I grow up' papers we had to write in school?"

"In first and second grade?" Jade nodded. "Sure, I remember them. They were fun."

Jade heard a "hmmp," but she chose to ignore it.

"What did you write about?" Jade looked at him, her curiosity obvious.

He didn't reply to her question, just glanced at her, striding along beside him.

"I suppose you always knew you wanted to be a dolphin trainer."

"Behaviorist." She grinned. "In elementary school, I just said I wanted to work with dolphins. Later, I learned about the various professional possibilities and the distinctions."

This time she was certain she heard him mumble "figures," as she kept pace beside him.

"What did you write about?" she asked.

She turned enough to catch sight of his face. Such a handsome face, his profile etched against the blue of the sky.

To her surprise, one side of his mouth pulled down.

"It doesn't matter. Come on. Let's get on back . . ."

But Jade knew that to Adam, it did indeed matter. She could, however, see his reluctance to discuss it, so she matched him stride for stride as he increased their pace.

They found the wooden railings at the petroglyph field crowded with visitors on their return trip, a tour group of Japanese tourists comprising most of it. A middle-aged woman in a muumuu stood to one side, speaking in Japanese while cameras flashed all along the railing.

Adam and Jade shared a smile as they walked by, glad they had started early and stopped on the way in. It had been special having the area to themselves.

The wind was picking up, blowing first one way, then another. They could not put their hats back on, even though the sun was high and the protection of a hat would have been welcome. There was no way to keep them on their heads. Jade's hair blew in all directions, more wisps escaping from her braid at every moment, fluttering against her cheeks and into her eyes. She patted and tucked the flyaways periodically, but it didn't seem to do any good.

Their pace increased yet again as they strode downhill, Adam allowing Jade to move ahead when they had to make room for a hiker going the other way.

Finally, they approached the trailhead.

"Where did you park?" Adam asked, moving back beside her for their last few minutes on the trail.

"Over in the hotel lot. I thought I'd take a swim before leaving." Her mischievous smile returned. "I shouldn't, really, since I'm not a hotel guest, but I know the lifeguard."

Adam laughed with her. "Tell you what. A swim sounds good. And I am a hotel guest, so you can be my guest."

"Thanks. I accept."

Together, they turned toward the main part of the hotel, Adam setting a slower pace as they started through the meandering gardens that surrounded the hotel. "We need to cool down."

The wind still blew, cooling their sweat-dampened bodies, and making the temperature seem lower than it actually was.

"This is nicer than the trail," Adam commented, ending several minutes of silence.

Jade looked about her at the lush garden and the rich green lawn. "You mean the garden path?"

Adam nodded. "After your comment Monday night, I made a point of exploring these gardens. You were right, they are beautiful. Whoever planned them knew what he—or she—" he added with a smile, "was doing. There are some fantastic plants. I especially like the fact that most of them are labeled with name-plates for those who aren't familiar with tropical plants."

"They spent a huge amount of money on plants when they built this hotel. A lot of the trees and plants they put in then were already mature plants that they bought from various parts of the islands. They paid premium prices to homeowners who were willing to part with rarer varieties of trees."

"Here's an interesting one." He stopped before a large woody shrub as tall as he was, with large white bell-shaped flowers.

"Angel's trumpet?" Jade asked. "Why is that interesting?"

"You see the sign? It says *Brugmansia candida.*"

Jade nodded, impressed by his easy pronunciation of the difficult scientific names.

"There's a question about whether the genus is *Brugmansia* or *Datura.* Some people still think *Brugmansia* is a section of *Datura.* It's a popular garden plant in the South, but extremely poisonous of course."

"Of course," Jade echoed. At least she did know that. "You know a lot about plants for a businessman."

Adam raised one eyebrow. "A businessman can't have other interests?"

Jade fumbled for an appropriate reply. "A businessman can be interested in anything he wants, I guess. It's just that you seem to be traveling all the time . . ."

"A happy circumstance for someone who is interested in botany."

"Botany," Jade said. "No offense, but you don't seem like the type." She softened her statement with a gentle smile.

Adam looked at her, his brows drawing together

over his nose. "What exactly is the botanical type? All kinds of people love to garden."

Jade laughed. "You've got me there. I'm not sure I really know. And I do know that anyone can enjoy gardening. I guess I wasn't necessarily associating a botanist with a gardener." She pulled the water bottle from her belt and took a drink, hoping to overcome her embarrassment. It didn't work. So she made another attempt to explain. "The word *botanist* just sounds so scientific. You look more like an athlete than a scientist."

She was glad to see that his response was a grin.

"You mean I don't look like a nerd."

She shrugged, but she grinned too.

"So you like to putter around in a garden? I used to love to do that when I was a kid, but it's been years since I had the time."

"That I can understand."

Now it was Jade's turn to feel nostalgic.

"My parents always had a large garden when I was growing up. Well, they still do. But when we were little, they would give each of us girls our own plot to care for. We could grow anything we wanted to." She sighed. "I haven't thought about that in years. It was a lot of fun."

Adam stepped off the garden path, heading toward a thick hedge of hybrid hibiscus that edged a curved section of grass. A statuette of an Indian goddess held court at the center of the small garden. Around her were hibiscus of all colors—huge blossoms a full eight inches across to small ones half that size. Flat petals, petals with curly edges; red and yellow, white and orange, pink and peach.

Adam stopped before the hedge, examining the variety of the blooms.

"I always thought I would become a scientist, develop new hybrids."

"Aha! So that's what you wrote about."

Chapter Six

It took Adam a moment to recall their earlier conversation about first grade essays and future professions.

He laughed, but the sound seemed forced.

"You've found me out."

Jade, however, was not to be deceived by his laughter.

"So what happened?"

Adam almost winced at the tone of her voice. The one thing he had never been able to abide was someone feeling sorry for him. He frowned.

"The family business is hotels and resorts."

He wasn't sure he wanted to tell her the whole truth. How his mother, in her final illness, had asked him to grant his father's deepest wish by trying the business. She knew he wanted to pursue science as a career; but she also knew how much his father hoped to bring his son into the company he'd worked so hard to build.

After his mother's plea, Adam changed his major from botany to hospitality.

But that was too personal. He couldn't share that with a woman he barely knew. He'd never shared it with anyone. Not even his father. He hardly wanted to admit it to himself.

So he shrugged. "It was always assumed I would go into the business with my father." He fingered the smooth petal of a peach hibiscus. The pastel tones darkened to a deep scarlet at the edge of the petal. "The botany was a childish thing, and eventually we have to put aside the things of a child."

Jade had to smile. "St. Paul's letter to the Corinthians."

Adam smiled back.

"It was a science project in the third grade that started it. I grew marigolds—some got more water than others."

"Hey, I did something like that once too. But I used green beans. And then I moved to experiments with fish." She grinned.

Adam grinned back. "I stuck with plants myself. I kept doing various projects with botany for the rest of my school years. Won some awards too. But once it was time for college, I chose hotel management."

Jade nodded. "Family tradition is important." As a Hawaiian, she could certainly relate to that.

They resumed their walk, moving away from the stunning hibiscus hedge.

Jade peered toward the main lobby, where the roof of the greenhouse atrium that gave the resort its name was visible. "So I guess you've seen the greenhouse?"

"Yes." Adam followed her line of vision. "I have to admit I first became interested in visiting here when I heard about the greenhouse atrium."

Jade pretended to be shocked. "Not the dolphins?"

She smiled as he shook his head slowly back and forth. That smile of hers could light up a room.

"So you're interested in orchids?"

"I'm interested in plants. But I love growing flowers and I've always been fascinated by orchids. It might go back to my youthful interest in mystery novels. Nero Wolfe was my hero."

"Really? Nero Wolfe? He's a detective, right? I think I've seen some TV shows about him."

"See? Didn't I tell you I was getting old?" His grin teased. "You don't even know about Nero Wolfe."

Jade dismissed this with a flick of her wrist.

"So, do you raise them?"

"Orchids? No, I don't raise anything. I move around a lot on business, and I finally had to give up trying. Plants require too much care. And they're almost impossible to move across international boundaries."

Jade flashed him a naughty grin. "You need to find a female customs agent. I'll bet you could charm your way right past her with a dozen orchid plants in your luggage."

Adam turned slowly toward her, one eyebrow raised. "My dear Ms. Kanahele. Was that a compliment?"

Jade drew her brows together in mock concentration. "Hmm. I think it might have been."

They both laughed. Jade realized she was having a

wonderful time. It was too easy to forget who Adam was, how her job might depend on his decisions for the hotel. Adam was so comfortable to be with, so easy to talk to. What a difference from her relationship with Teddy.

But it also kept getting in the way of her stated purpose in socializing with Adam. She was having so much fun, she kept forgetting that she was supposed to be gleaning information for Dolphin Life Research.

By the time they reached the pool, they were more than ready for a cooling swim.

It wasn't difficult for Adam to talk Jade into lunch afterward. But Jade admitted she would feel strange eating at the Thatched Hut—it was too close to the dolphin pool and her coworkers.

So he took her to the resort's golf club where they ate on a terrace overlooking the starting tee. The early morning cloud cover had dissipated with the wind, leaving Mauna Kea clear for its entire length. It towered above them, a glint from one of the observatories gleaming at its summit.

"I heard you can take horseback rides up the mountain."

Jade shrugged. "I wouldn't be surprised. Might not be that mountain, though. I think the hotel works with a ranch in the Kohala mountains."

"And where would that be?"

Jade pointed to the north, toward an area heavily banked with clouds. "The Kohala mountains get quite a bit of rain."

"That doesn't sound like a good thing when it comes to trail rides."

Adam's eyebrow climbed upward. He was surprised to see Jade swallow at the gesture. Perhaps the old pirate hadn't lost his touch after all.

Then she grinned and it was his turn to swallow.

"It keeps you cool."

Adam laughed, but his laughter faded quickly when Jade's expression turned somber and she asked her next question.

"So, are you regretting that you didn't become a botanist after all?"

Adam put his sandwich back on his plate. "Isn't that a little personal?"

Jade shrugged. If she felt bad for intruding in a private matter, she didn't look regretful. She merely took another bite from her club sandwich and chewed slowly, looking up at him through those impossibly long lashes.

"I'm not the one dreading my thirtieth birthday."

"I'm not dreading it." He kept his voice steady and free of emotion.

"How do you like your job? With your father's company, I mean?"

"I like my job. I get to visit beautiful places and meet all kinds of people."

Even with the table between them, he heard Jade's sigh.

"You should be able to say 'I love my job.'"

That wrung a smile from him.

"I have a surprise for you, Jade. Our world is far from ideal."

Finishing the last of her sandwich, Jade shook her head slowly back and forth. "Our world is what we make it." Her eyes locked on his. "If you really want to be a botanist, you can still go back to school. It's never too late. You're young, despite your thirtieth birthday."

"I like my job, Jade. I get to travel to interesting locations, and see a lot of beautiful gardens and new varieties of plants. I find the challenge of saving a hotel stimulating."

Adam picked up his sandwich again.

"And I don't consider myself old." His voice was firm, his tone putting an end to the discussion. Or so he thought.

"But you wanted to create new plants. It's not quite the same, is it?"

"Father!" Adam's voice reflected his surprise at seeing his parent standing at his hotel room door.

Warren Donovan smiled at his son. "Surprised, are you?"

Adam returned a wry smile. "You might say that. Checking up on me, are you?"

Warren chuckled; Adam knew he would enjoy the phrasing that echoed his own.

"Of course not. I have every confidence in you. I just happened to be passing through Hawaii on my way home from Tokyo and thought I'd take a look at this property you're so interested in. I must say the Japanese love visiting Hawaii, and Hawaiian weddings are still big business with them. There was a lot of interest in whether or not we'd be expanding over here."

As they spoke, Warren moved into the room. Adam relieved him of his suitcase, even though it was only a carryon style bag with wheels.

Warren took in his son, his eyes lingering on Adam's face and its wary expression.

"I also wanted to be here to wish my only son a happy birthday on Wednesday."

Adam found himself momentarily speechless. They were not a sentimental family, the Donovans. So this sudden visit and its purported reason were a definite surprise.

Warren, similarly discomfited by his admission, moved farther into the room, taking in the casual décor. While some of the local hotels went in for the more formal territorial style of furniture, the Orchid House employed a tropical vacation theme. Bamboo and wicker, heavy sisal mats on the floor, watercolors of local flowers, seashells under glass—those were the things that adorned their rooms and suites. And, of course, a blooming orchid plant in every room.

"I haven't seen much of the property yet, but I must say the island is everything you claimed."

Adam's mouth tightened. While he expected to have to prove himself to others in the company, he thought his own father would have faith in his abilities.

In his usual irritating manner, his father seemed to read his mind.

"I'm not questioning your business acumen, Adam. You've already proved that you know this business. And very well too. I merely wanted to stop here for a few days to recoup." He lowered himself into a chair with a sigh. His head lay back against the plump upholstered pillows, and his arms rested on the thick bamboo arms. "I'm not as young as I used to be. Crossing the date line gets harder every year."

Adam laughed. "Father, you may not be as young as you used to be, but you are definitely not old. However, I don't blame you for stopping here to rest. Those time changes from the east can be a killer no matter how old you are. How long are you staying?"

Warren shrugged. "Not too long. We'll spend a few days together, I'll take you out for your birthday, then leave shortly afterward. I can't really take more time than that."

Adam made a sound that could have been a snort. "You have the best staff in the world, Father. You could take off a month and everything would run smoothly."

"Perhaps. I may actually test that out soon." He grinned, sitting up in his chair. "I have a friend—a . . . a woman—coming to join me here for a few days. I hope you don't mind."

Adam's brow shot up in surprise. Ever since his mother died the summer he graduated from high school, his father had devoted every moment to his company. Adam often wondered if he did it because he found it fulfilling, or if he was merely using it to keep his grief at bay.

His parents had had a tremendous marriage. Adam often wondered if the deep love his parents shared was the reason he himself was still unmarried. He had yet to find someone he could view in the same way his father had viewed his mother.

Warren had cherished his wife, sharing every aspect of his life with her. They had done everything together—run the business, socialized, shared interests and hobbies.

So far, Adam had met women he could respect in the business world, women he could enjoy shared interests and hobbies with, women he could have fun with at social gatherings. There had not been anyone with whom he could share all three.

"Why would I mind?" Actually, he thought, it was about time his father had a girlfriend.

Warren chuckled. "Well, it is *your* birthday."

Yes, here he was, almost thirty. He would like to settle down. His parents had been married for years by the time his father reached his thirtieth birthday. But marrying wasn't as easy as deciding it was time. Over the years he'd also been plagued with women who were more interested in the Donovan name and the Donovan fortune than in Adam himself.

"So who is she?" He hoped Warren wouldn't fall for a young, unscrupulous type. An older, successful man like Warren was a prime target for a certain type of predatory female.

Warren almost looked embarrassed, a novel situation for Adam. It also set off alarm bells. Adam could imagine him being embarrassed if he had to admit to his son that he was marrying someone young enough to be his daughter.

"You know, I loved your mother very much."

Adam nodded. There was never any question in his mind that his parents had been deeply in love. "I know that. But Mother's been gone for over ten years. I'm sure she would want you to be happy." Happy, but not foolish.

Warren seemed relieved to hear Adam's words.

"Do you remember Anne Hollister, the assistant manager at the resort on Virgin Gorda?"

Adam remembered. He'd looked into the feasibility of acquiring a resort property on Virgin Gorda in the Virgin Islands several years ago. It was a tremendous location, lots of acreage, beautiful views. After researching the resort and the area, he'd recommended acquisition by Donovan Enterprises. One of the assets he'd listed in his report was the assistant manager, a woman named Anne Hollister. She was an excellent manager, had great people skills. She could have been a successful member of the diplomatic corps. He'd suggested that she be offered a job in the restructured complex as general manager.

"Didn't she become general manager?"

"You know she did. On your recommendation." Warren gave his son a guarded smile. "I've been visiting there for the past couple of years. Keeping up with the renovations, you know."

Adam laughed. "Okay."

Warren seemed flustered. Adam guessed it was difficult to discuss such issues with your offspring. He didn't suppose it became easier when said offspring were adults.

"Anne is a wonderful woman," Warren continued. "We had a lot of meetings, and they sometimes lasted through mealtimes. Soon I was asking her to meet me for dinner, taking her dancing afterward." He smiled. "It's always a good thing to check out the competition. See what they're offering."

"Of course." Adam replied seriously, but he was smiling inside. He couldn't think of a better match for his father than Anne. They both lived for the hotel business. "I suppose you took her to all the other resorts in the area to check out the dining facilities and look into the type of entertainment offered."

His father smiled. "Don't get smart with your old man, son."

"I take it things have gotten serious?"

Warren's smile dissolved. Once again he seemed on edge.

"I've been thinking of asking Anne to marry me. But I wanted to speak to you first. It seemed the proper thing to do."

Adam walked up to his father and clapped his hand on his shoulder. "I think it's wonderful, Father. I hope you two have a lot of happy years together."

Warren seemed relieved. "I wasn't sure how you'd feel about it. Someone taking your mother's place, you know."

"I suppose that could be a problem with a young child, but I'm a grown-up." Adam frowned, wondering if his father still thought of him as a child. "Did you really think I'd object to you finding happiness with a wonderful woman like Anne? I think it's great; you should have found someone years ago." Adam opened the small refrigerator in the room's bar, checking the bottles inside for something they could use for a celebratory toast. "I wouldn't object to anyone you wanted to marry, as long as she made you happy. What have you done about female companionship all these years, anyway?"

Adam was naturally curious, but his father's reticence quickly asserted itself.

"None of your business, young man."

Adam laughed, pushing the refrigerator door closed. "There's nothing in here suitable for a toast. We'll have to call room service for some champagne."

Warren waved away the suggestion. "Why don't we wait until dinner?"

"Fine."

The toast didn't matter. Adam just wanted his father to know that he was happy for him. This explained his father's little visit. Adam's birthday was merely an excuse—Warren wanted to tell him about Anne.

Far from leaving him disillusioned, Adam was relieved to fit Warren back into his proper slot—a workaholic focused on current and future business. It was his father's devotion to Donovan Enterprises that left Adam feeling lacking. Adam worked hard, felt he was an asset to the company. Yet he constantly second-guessed himself and his abilities because he couldn't seem to live up to his father's example.

And then there were the other employees who watched his every move, hoping to find something to support their theory that he had an important job with the firm merely because his father was the CEO.

So, despite the upcoming engagement, Adam couldn't help suspecting that Warren might mean to check up on him.

"Did you introduce yourself to management?"

"No, I did not. I said I was joining my son who was already staying here. I assumed you would have a suite."

Warren was interrupted by a knock at the door. Adam answered, and a young man entered, dressed in white slacks and a purple Hawaiian shirt printed with orchids. He held a cellophane wrapped basket of fruit in his hands.

"With the compliments of the management, sir."

He set the fruit basket on the coffee table. Adam thanked him and walked him to the door, slipping a folded bill into his hand. The young man gave him a wide smile.

"*Mahalo,* sir."

When Adam returned, Warren was taking a card with his name on it from the basket. "Well, it seems management knows I'm here after all."

At that, Adam laughed, a hearty release that calmed any remaining tension between them. "I hate to take away from your ego, Father, but every guest gets one of these as a welcome gift."

Warren nodded, a pleased look on his face. "A very nice touch. It has class. Still, gestures like that can be expensive."

Adam agreed, but he didn't want to get into it just now. His father claimed he was there for his birthday; he would try to enjoy his visit, not second-guess his every statement.

"Come on, Father." Adam clapped him on the back. "The best way I know to relax is to stretch out next to the pool. They have books and newspapers down there you can borrow. Go put on your swim trunks and let's go."

Adam gripped the handle of the suitcase and escorted Warren to the door of the suite's second bedroom. He paused on the threshold, putting his hand on his father's arm.

"It's good to see you again, Father."

"And you, son."

Warren covered Adam's hand with his own, holding it there against his forearm. They looked briefly into each other's eyes.

Adam was the first to turn away. He often wished that they were a more demonstrative family. He sometimes thought it would be nice to throw his arms around his father and envelope him in a bear hug. Since he was two inches taller and some fifty pounds heavier than Warren, he could do it too. But while the *idea* held some appeal, the reality—and the change from the status quo—was too much for him. There were too many years of handshakes and fatherly pats on the back to overcome.

With a shrug, Adam entered his own room. He'd see if he could get Warren to relax. He'd be doing Anne a favor.

"What do you hear from the girls?"

Dinner was over and Carol and Frank Kanahele were settling down in front of the television, preparing to watch their favorite weekly drama. Frank sat at the end of the sofa, his arm lying along the back edge, ready to drop onto his wife's shoulder. As soon as she stopped fussing with the magazines on the coffee table and sat down.

His question did the trick. Carol turned, smiling broadly.

"Our jewels?"

Her voice teased. Frank had had doubts about naming their daughters after gemstones. It was an idea Carol had when she was pregnant with their second child. With their eldest daughter named Jade, she wanted to chose another "jewel" girl's name. Frank prayed for a boy, but finally agreed to Momi, Hawaiian for pearl. Momi was a popular island name and the combination of Jade and Momi was not as "cute" as Jade and Pearl. Three years later, he decided not to argue, and let Carol have her first choice, Ruby.

He had a great-aunt on the mainland named Ruby, so it could be considered a family name. Carol, however, loved equating her daughters with gems and used the obvious references often.

Now she sat beside Frank, snuggling into his embrace.

"Ruby is all settled in with cousin Clarice. Clarice says she loves having such an energetic young person around. Says it makes her feel young too."

Frank murmured something unintelligible, but Carol offered her agreement anyway and continued.

"Ruby is helping her with the yard work too. They're planting a garden."

Frank nodded. "All the girls used to enjoy gardening until they got so busy with schoolwork and extracurricular activities. Ruby will have a good time."

Carol captured Frank's free hand in both of hers. This was the kind of relationship she wanted for her girls.

"Momi starts classes next week. She says the apartment is nice and very convenient. She also says her roommate was a good choice because she likes to cook. She's going to try and teach Momi."

"That should be interesting," Frank commented. "At least we won't have to sample the results."

Carol slapped his arm lightly in playful rebuke. "Shame on you. One day Momi will be an excellent cook. She just has to set her mind to do it."

Frank kept his eyes safely on the television screen, even though it was showing an especially irritating commercial.

"Jade loves her job, as you know. She called last night when you were bowling and told me about the work she's been doing. She does love working with the children who come in from the local schools."

"She'll be a wonderful mother someday." Frank squeezed Carol's shoulder. "Did she say anything more about the hotel manager?"

"No, nothing." Carol frowned. "She said something about going on a hike with a hotel guest she met at that reception she told us about."

Frank frowned. "Someone from the mainland? Did she say anything else about him?"

"No." Carol held tightly to Frank's hand. "You don't think the quilt would find her a true love from the mainland, do you?"

"Now, honey." Frank ran his hand lightly up and down Carol's upper arm. "You'll have to let go of your jewels one of these days. And Jade hasn't lived at home much these last few years."

"I know, I know. But when she traveled to do her studies, we always knew she'd be coming back here eventually. If she falls in love with someone from the mainland, she might move away forever." Carol tucked her head into her husband's shoulder and sighed heavily. "I never thought the quilt would find her someone from far away."

Frank placed a soft kiss on her forehead. "I'm sure everything will work out. You'll have to have faith in Helen."

Chapter Seven

It had been a long morning. Jade hadn't gotten enough rest the night before, her slumber interrupted by another strangely disturbing dream that she thought involved Adam Donovan. If only she could remember her dreams!

Now, at the end of a frustrating morning, she trudged through the resort gardens on her way to lunch. Her feet felt heavy, as though encased in thick-soled hiking boots. Yet they were clad in her usual workday rubber slippers, the inexpensive flip-flops everyone in the islands wore to the beach—and most other places besides.

She'd just had the worst swim with the dolphins session of her life. One of the hotel lottery winners, a man, didn't want to follow directions. He seemed to think that winning the chance to participate in the swim session meant he could just get into the water with the animals and do whatever he wanted. He'd gotten aggressive and verbally abusive to the point that Ryan had to lead him out of the lagoon and get a security guard to escort him away. Jade found the ordeal terribly upsetting, and was glad she had the first lunch break.

The beautifully landscaped grounds soothed her battered spirits, much as swimming with the dolphins replenished her spiritual side. How long could anyone continue to feel stressed when faced with blooming hibiscus bushes, ripe with primary colors. Bougainvillea vines in tangerine and scarlet and magenta. Creamy white spider lilies and angelwing jasmine. Fragrant gardenias, tiare, and tuberose.

Jade passed a solemn, squat Buddha as she headed for the small square of grassy lawn that overlooked a flock of pink flamingos. It was her favorite spot for lunch—a quiet, private place where she could watch the pink birds and unwind as she ate. Her footsteps already felt lighter and the tension was seeping from her body.

As she rounded a bend in the path, Jade was disappointed to see someone already occupying her retreat. A man was sitting cross-legged in the grass, his broad back to her. His broad *bare* back—a vision of tanned perfection. Was he sunbathing? A strange place and stranger position.

And there was something familiar about that back.

His head came up as Jade stepped off the path and onto the grass, and she realized who it was. That head of thick wheat-colored hair could only belong to Adam.

She advanced quietly, so as not to disturb him, curious to see what he was doing. It seemed a strange place for sunbathing when there were three pools and a beach in the resort complex. And most of the rooms had patios or balconies, suitable for private sun-bathing.

Changing the angle of her approach, Jade realized that he was sketching. There was a pad of paper in his lap, his concentration on a grouping of small plants before him. Was Adam an artist? He'd revealed several things of a personal nature to her, but not that.

Jade raised her neck, trying to peer over his shoulder. She really wanted to see what was on that paper.

Adam left his father perusing the Wall Street Journal at the pool, sneaking off to the garden for some R & R.

Rest and relaxation were not in abundant supply when Warren Donovan and Adam were together. Two strong personalities, each with definite ideas for accomplishing similar goals, father and son often clashed. After two days of his father's company, Adam needed a break—a break from everything associated with his father.

So he played a strenuous game of tennis with the resort pro then grabbed his sketchbook and found a private spot in the garden. He needed a stretch of quiet.

The resort did have amazing gardens, as well as the unique orchid greenhouse atrium. The gardens covered acres of the property, with wings of guest rooms integrated among them.

He'd strolled for a while, until the beauty of the surroundings seeped into his soul and he felt the tensions of family and corporate life ease.

Finally, he'd stopped before a grouping of devil flower, a truly unusual plant with blackish-maroon flowers. "Tacca chantrierorum," the sign beside it read, "Family Taccaceae." Adam had seen them once before, on a visit to Malaya. The strange blossom looked like a cross between a trillium and a Lady's Slipper—one that had failed. Its strange color was, of course, the reason for its odd name, but Adam preferred the alternate designation "bat flower." He thought it more appropriate as the blossom looked somewhat like that nocturnal creature.

Removing his shirt, he settled comfortably on the grass before the grouping of plants. Not too close—the flower had a disagreeable, rotten smell. But it was an interesting subject for a sketch.

He added lines for the long drooping filiform inner bracts and frowned at the paper. He hadn't gotten the inner, helmet-shaped stamens exactly right.

He must have been in a deep state of concentration, because he was unaware of Jade's presence until she spoke.

"Wow" was her one-word greeting. She stood in the grass, beside and slightly behind him, her eyes intent on the sketchbook in his lap. Her gaze moved between the drawing and the plant, and back again. "I knew you said you were interested in plants, but I had no idea you were such an artist."

Adam merely shrugged. He preferred to keep this side of himself private, but it was too late for that now and he wasn't one to cry over spilled milk. He rose to his feet, holding on to the sketchbook while grabbing his T-shirt off the ground.

"It's part of the scientific method—you have to be able to sketch the things you're studying."

Jade stood beside him, interested eyes still focused on his sketchbook. "True, but nowadays you can take a photograph, put it on the computer, and tinker with it for the best clarity and color."

Her practical attitude brought a grin to his lips.

"And you call yourself a scientist?"

Any resentment he might have felt at her intrusion into his private world fled when he looked closer. There were fine lines etched into the skin beside her eyes, and none of her usual sparkle showed in their depths. That vitality was so much a part of her, he found himself anxious to find the cause of its loss.

For the first time since his high school days, a woman of his acquaintance was learning of his obsession with sketching plants, and it didn't make him want to run and hide. In fact, he was eager to distract her by sharing his sketches.

And even more eager to discover why she was wandering in the garden in the middle of the day, looking so dejected.

Within minutes, Adam had pulled on his shirt and invited Jade to join him on one of the shaded benches. They sat side by side, thighs almost touching on the short bench.

The midday sun filtering through the lacy branches of a tall silk oak tree warmed them; a light breeze rustled the leaves overhead and ruffled their hair. Adam turned back the pages of his sketchbook and shared an intimate part of his life with this woman he'd known for only a week.

Their two heads, one dark, one light, touched softly as they bent over the pages. Jade didn't say much after her initial raptures, but Adam knew she appreciated the drawings by her gentle sighs of appreciation.

"Oh, Adam, these orchid sketches are absolutely beautiful. They should be made into note cards or something. Everyone would want them."

Adam laughed. It felt good hearing her high opinion of his sketches. He knew she was sincere, but he also knew he wasn't interested in commercializing his talent.

"It's just a hobby."

He lifted his hand, running his fingers lightly along the side of her face, over the lines that bracketed her eyes.

"Something's bothering you. You don't usually have these."

His hand passed reassuringly over her shoulder as he brought it back to his side. "Want to talk about it?"

Jade released a deep sigh. "Maybe."

Adam waited, anxious to hear her story, but only when the time was right for her.

Jade flipped another page in the sketchbook, taking a moment to examine a clump of hanging mangoes.

"Not a flower," she commented, but he noted the lack of a grin. Or even a smile.

"But still a botanical specimen," he said.

Jade continued to stare at the pencil sketch.

"I had a rough morning," she finally said, adding a frustrated sigh. "It's the kind of thing that's to be expected when you work with the public, I guess. But it's my first experience of the sort, and it was upsetting."

She proceeded to tell him about the unpleasant guest.

"That's why I came this way. I love this spot." She gestured around them, at the grassy lawn, the numerous flowering plants, and the funky pink birds visible from the carefully placed benches. "I love the flamingos. I come here for my breaks or lunch hour when I need a little time alone."

"And I was here instead."

Jade turned toward him, her eyes intense with feeling. "You helped make everything okay." Color seeped into her cheeks as she dropped her eyelids and admitted, "You're even better than the flamingos."

Touched by her words, Adam tipped her head back up with a finger under her chin. He met her emotional stare with one of his own. There was passion in this small woman, and much as he wanted to, he didn't know if he was ready to face it.

He ran his thumb gently across her chin, then up and over her lower lip. Jade swallowed hard, but returned his caress with a light kiss on the pad of his thumb.

It was Adam's turn to swallow hard. He was almost relieved when Jade grasped his hand, then held it captive on the bench between them. She turned her attention back to the sketchbook in her lap.

"Thank you for showing me your sketches, Adam."

"You're welcome."

Carefully, she closed the book.

"I have to get back to work. We take turns having lunch." She looked back up at him. "Our visit was probably more therapeutic than just coming here to sit for an hour. Thank you."

Adam suddenly realized that she'd come for lunch and never had any. "But you didn't have anything to eat."

"I wasn't hungry." Jade handed him the sketchbook.

Adam accepted the book, reluctant to have to part from Jade after so short a time. But it was a working day, and he didn't want to be the cause of any problems for her.

He rose with a quick upward thrust of his powerful leg muscles, then reached down to help Jade to her feet. Jade's startled gaze flew upward, and he saw her blink, then swallow. Her cheeks pinkened in a most appealing manner, and she placed her hand in his.

Adam felt the warm pressure of her hand as it settled into his. It was small and dainty, like Jade herself. Yet it was warm and so alive, its vitality transferred into his hand, then moved into his body. It energized him. He could face anything with her hand in his—his tiresome birthday, his father's questions, his time-consuming job.

They stood for a moment, her hand held tenderly in his, their eyes staring, blue into brown. They seemed drawn together, leaning inexorably nearer, his head moving ever closer to hers.

The moment their lips touched was magical. Adam

had wondered if it could match that last brief touching of lips, that tender sampling on the bluff overlooking the ocean.

Now he knew. It didn't match it. It far surpassed that first experience.

His lips pressed softly against hers, feeling the warm satin of her lips. Her lips were firm and trembled slightly beneath his; even without the salt spray, she tasted of the sea.

Suddenly, voices intruded into their private haven. Warned of an interruption, Adam and Jade sprang apart putting a respectable distance between their bodies.

The voices preceded a family group moving along the garden path. Curious rapid thumps were quickly replaced by the figure of a small boy in tennis shoes, hopping his way up the trail.

"I'm a bunny, Mommy, I'm a bunny."

A young couple followed a few steps behind, glancing over at Jade and Adam with a smile and a shrug. The boy continued to hop until he disappeared from sight, his parents following.

Adam watched the couple, aware of Jade beside him, who picked up his sketchbook and handed it back over to his care. He was careful not to look into her face, afraid of the regret she might be feeling over their kiss.

But the brush of her hand against his as he took the book removed any uncertainties on that regard. Her fingers lingered against his wrist, telegraphing clearer than any words her feelings on that subject.

Adam finally met her eyes, grinning widely at the shy smile on her face.

"I guess I'd better get going," she said. She brushed her fingers against his hand once more. "My lunch hour is over."

Adam grinned as he watched her head off toward the lagoon. He wondered if he looked the way Jade had that first morning when he'd seen her coming in to work. Because he finally thought he knew how she must have felt.

Jade got through the rest of the afternoon with her usual optimistic attitude firmly back in place. Her quiet luncheon talk with Adam had been enough to refresh her spirits. But that kiss! The brief kiss they'd shared on the bluff last week had been very nice. Special even. But this one . . .

Jade had been kissed before, and usually enjoyed the act very much. But a kiss from Adam Donovan was surely something extra special. Her heartbeat accelerated, her blood seemed to hum through her veins.

She'd planned to read a new novel she'd just gotten from the library that evening, but she found herself unable to concentrate on the book. The hero seemed arrogant and vain, the heroine shallow. Adam was so much better in all respects than the man in the story, who was vicious in the business world, and cold toward the heroine when they first met.

Jade frowned at the book. At least she didn't think

Adam was like the fictional hero. But she didn't know, did she? The attraction between them was so powerful she was constantly distracted from trying to extract information about the hotel from him. She still didn't know what his business at the resort actually involved. And she still knew precious little about him.

Jade tossed the highly anticipated novel aside. Maybe she'd try it again in a few months.

She was trying to decide between scrubbing the bathtub and cleaning out the refrigerator when the phone rang and saved her from either task. Her sister Momi was on the line, eager for an update on the antique quilt and her dating situation. They had barely exchanged greetings when Momi posed her first question.

"So, how was the hike with Adam?"

Jade was surprised Momi even remembered his name. "It was fine. I enjoyed it."

What an understatement! She was glad there was no video cam attached to the phone. She was sure her whole face must be bright red.

"So, is the relationship moving along then?"

"Relationship? There's no relationship!"

Momi laughed. "Methinks the lady doth protest too much," she said, in her own version of the famous line from *Hamlet*.

"Anyway, maybe I just have more faith in Mom's quilt than you do."

Jade groaned. "I forgot about the quilt."

"How could you forget something like that!"

Momi's voice rose so high Jade pulled the receiver away from her ear.

"I have other things on my mind." Jade recalled that terrific kiss. Then the worry over the sale of the hotel. Yes, she had a lot of things cluttering her mind these days.

"Things like a guy named Adam?"

Momi's voice had returned to normal, but Jade felt her cheeks burn at her sister's accurate guess.

"So, tell me. Have you been seeing him? Besides the hike, I mean."

"Yes and no."

"Huh?"

"Well, I have been *seeing* him. He's always around the hotel. But we haven't had any official dates. I'm trying to get to know him so that I can find out what he might be planning for the hotel. And maybe influence his decisions about dolphin programs."

"You're *using* him?" Momi seemed shocked.

"That sounds so crass." But of course it was true. Jade frowned.

"Is this a case of the end justifying the means?"

"I guess so. If I can save our dolphins from the stress-related illnesses common in animals forced to interact with too many humans, then yes, it is worth it."

Momi clicked her tongue. "That's not a very nice thing to do if he is the one the quilt brought you."

Jade sucked in her breath. Momi didn't really believe that nonsense, did she?

126

"But that whole thing about the quilt is so ridiculous," Jade insisted.

"Why?" Momi's voice was dead serious.

Jade, her mouth open to reply, stopped. It just was, that's all. Because love potions were ridiculous, just as good luck tokens were. They were all superstitious nonsense, and Jade was too modern to believe in any of it.

"Just think about it, Jade. You've always believed in the family *'aumakua*. And isn't the *mana* in the quilt the same kind of thing?"

"Not at all."

But Momi broke in quickly. "Yes. It is. Both are tied in with old Hawaiian culture. It's part of our heritage."

Jade had to get her away from this line of questioning.

"Still, I haven't been dating him. I just see him around. And we've had a meal together now and again."

"That seems promising," Momi said. "So, do you like him?"

But instead of an answer, Jade almost groaned into the phone. "Oh, Momi, I am so confused."

Momi had the audacity to laugh.

"Well, I'm glad you think it's funny." Jade didn't find her confusion laughable.

"No, it's not that. I was just thinking that maybe Mom's quilt is working its magic after all."

"What!"

How did they get back to that?

"Face it, Jade. You met him right after Mom gave you the quilt. Now you're all upset and confused. I mean, I just asked a nice simple question: Do you like him? And what do I get? A big groan and a confession that you're all confused. Doesn't that sound like love?"

"Love?"

Although Jade thought about Adam all the time—and she had certainly loved their two brief kisses—she had not thought in terms of love. Not love between the two of them. Just the word itself was scary.

"Think about it. Even from the little you told me about him and your relationship, it sounds to me like you're crazy about him. As far as I'm concerned, crazy and love are just about the same thing."

Jade groaned. Again.

"Yeah. I thought so."

"But Momi . . . you remember Teddy."

An indecipherable noise from the opposite end of the line told her that Momi did remember her last boyfriend.

"You know, he and Adam have quite a bit in common," Jade remarked.

Momi seemed to consider this for a moment.

"No, I don't think so. Not from what you've told me."

"They're both rich *haoles*. How can I have anything in common with Adam? You know what happened when Teddy introduced me to his parents."

What a disaster that had been! His upper-crust parents took one look at Jade in her bright Hawaiian-print dress and were hard pressed to maintain their smiles. She was sure they pulled Teddy aside as soon as possible and told him she was totally unsuitable. Their family could trace their lineage back three hundred years, to a Duke of York, and hence to an English king.

In any case, Teddy, who had sworn he would love her for all eternity, broke off their relationship soon afterward. His reasons were vague—something about not rushing into things, and getting serious about his studies. He'd left the University of Hawaii at the end of the term and transferred to the college his parents had preferred all along. And Jade had battled self-image problems around mainlanders ever since.

"But from what you told me about Teddy, all you really had in common were mutual friends at school."

Jade groaned.

"What do you and Adam talk about?" Momi asked. "Is it just the resort? Because then you might have a problem."

Jade thought back over their time together. While they did spend a lot of time talking about the resort—and she spent a great deal of time speaking about dolphins—they touched on numerous other subjects as well.

When she spoke, her voice was slow, considering.

"I think we have some mutual interests besides the resort. We both like to swim and hike."

"I don't think this is another Teddy, Jade. He was pretty shallow, you know. I never told you, but he hit on me once when we were all at a party together. I didn't like him at all, but I didn't want to upset you by telling you about it. Then his parents came to visit, and it all worked itself out."

They spoke for a few minutes longer, then Jade hung up the phone. Her thoughts were in a jumble. She'd tried so hard not to think about Teddy after he left her, that she hadn't been able to see the deeper reasons for their problems. All she'd been able to see these past weeks were the superficial similarities between him and Adam. The money. The socially prominent family.

At least, she assumed the Donovans were socially prominent. It usually went with the bank balance. There wasn't any way for her to determine what Adam would be like around his family, though, unless they were with him in her presence. She'd just have to try and look deeper into his psyche. She didn't want to risk another disaster. Adam didn't act like a snob, but then neither had Teddy. Until his parents turned up.

Then there was the quilt. Could Momi be right about it? There was a certain logic to her argument.

What was she thinking? She was a scientist. She didn't believe in esoteric love potions, no matter how steeped in tradition.

Hina padded up, placing her soft paws on Jade's thigh and rubbing her head against her upper arm. Jade gathered the cat into her lap.

"What do you think, Hina? Could there really be powerful *mana* in that quilt of ours? Did Grandmother Helen help me meet Adam?"

She rubbed her cheek against the silky gray fur of Hina's head.

"Is he my true love?"

Hina's answering "meow" startled Jade into a nervous laugh. But somehow Helen and Hina's support made the thought of love less scary. Thinking she might be falling in love with a man she'd known for less than two weeks didn't seem as harebrained ridiculous if she could somehow tie it in with the influence of her ancestor.

Taking Hina into her arms, Jade walked into the bedroom and stood beside the bed. The red leaves and flowers spread across the white fabric, looking brighter tonight in the artificial light.

"I wish you could talk to me, Grandmother Helen. The way you did to Thomas."

She'd no sooner said the words than Jade felt a shiver up her spine. Perhaps Helen *had* spoken to her, she thought. Those strange dreams she'd been having. They usually came on nights when she unknowingly pulled the quilt over her.

Walking back into the living room, Jade fell into an overstuffed chair she'd acquired when her Aunty Laura bought a new one. With Hina still cuddled in her arms, she thought back over the series of dreams. Most of them were hazy memories of dolphins that made her feel good upon awakening. Some, she knew, had involved Adam, but those were less clear and more troublesome.

The loud rumble of a purr integrated with the music

of a slack key guitar coming from the CD player. Jade looked down into the gray furry face snuggled against her shoulder.

"What would happen if I slept under the quilt tonight, Hina? On purpose." The thought was both scary and exciting.

Jade couldn't wait for bedtime.

Tuesday was Jade's next day off from Dolphin Life Research. But recently her days off had been spent moonlighting for her cousin's business concern, Sea Explorations. Keoki was shorthanded until all the college students returned for the summer. So Jade was filling in for him on her days off, leading hotel guests out for a trek in an outrigger canoe, topped off with an hour of snorkeling. She enjoyed the work, loved teaching the tourists—especially the teens—about the island's sea life. But today she wondered if she wouldn't have preferred sleeping in and just doing some simple housecleaning activities.

She'd slept beneath Helen's quilt the night before, and she wanted time to think about the dream she could only vaguely remember. However, a promise was a promise, so she'd gotten herself up and dressed, and was now busy readying the canoe for a snorkeling trek. Moki, her fellow guide, checked their equipment, while she stowed some bottles of water in the canoe.

"Hey, Jade."

Jade's head snapped up at the familiar voice. She was smiling almost before she met the eyes of Adam

Donovan, who looked especially well this morning in navy swim trunks and a yellow T-shirt. There was another man behind him who looked like an older version of Adam—handsome, clear blue eyes, hair still thick and wavy but mostly silver. He too wore a pair of swim trunks and a T-shirt.

He must be Adam's father, Jade realized—the man who owned the resorts!

Jade felt her heart stop. For a full five seconds, she was sure it did not beat at all.

Then she forced her eyes back to Adam.

"Hi. Going for a swim?"

Adam smiled. "Going snorkeling."

His grin broadened as her eyes widened in surprise. "Snorkeling?"

Once again her eyes moved to the older version of Adam. She'd have to meet his father! She took a deep steadying breath. She could not allow Teddy and the insecurities he'd left in her to dictate her reaction now. This was an opportunity for her; a chance to speak to Mr. Donovan himself, the CEO and largest shareholder of Donovan Enterprises, according to the information garnered by Tami and Ryan.

She smiled, hoping it was friendly and natural.

"Jade," Adam said, "I'd like you to meet my father, Warren Donovan. He's passing through the islands, and I thought I'd show him a few of the sights. And it seemed like snorkeling was a must-do activity."

"Oh, it is."

Jade thrust out her hand, then wondered if that was

too forward. Teddy's parents had not thought her feminine enough. Apparently feminine and demure were synonymous in their world. And Jade, always a tomboy, had never been demure.

But she had often been complimented for her smile.

She smiled at Adam's father. "Mr. Donovan. Nice to meet you."

"Please. Call me Warren. You wouldn't want to make me feel old, would you?"

He winked at her, and Jade relaxed. She noticed that his eyes were as blue as his son's and his smile as devastating. She hoped he would be as easy to talk to. She could do some major lobbying. What better way to let someone know the hazards of certain practices, than to showcase the animals in the wild? She hoped they would see dolphins on their excursion.

"I take it you're our morning clients."

"Yep." Adam's grin teased her. "You told me you worked here, remember? So I told Father we had to arrange to have you for a guide. After all, how many people get to go out snorkeling with a real marine biologist?"

Jade laughed. "Yeah, I should make Keoki pay me extra for filling in here. His clients get all the benefits of my extensive and expensive education."

She called Moki over, introducing him to the Donovans before she sent them to the Sea Explorations counter to take care of the paperwork.

As Jade watched the two men move toward the low building, some of her previous night's dream came back to her. She and Adam had been on the beach. She looked around her, but she didn't think the resort's beach was the one in the dream. That beach had been all smooth white sand, not gray-looking sand strewn with black and white rocks.

Squinting her eyes as she tried to focus on the hazy images, Jade saw two figures moving together, she and Adam, arms around one another, their bodies moving as one.

Then, before she could come to any conclusion about what it all meant, the images faded, and Moki called out to her.

Chapter Eight

The snorkeling trek was a success. Not all the guests wanted to help row, and Jade and Moki often did all the work themselves. But both Adam and Warren took up oars and seemed to enjoy the experience. Their powerful strokes got them to the snorkeling site in record time.

Viewing at the site was excellent. They'd chosen a coral reef which attracted schools of yellow butterfly and tiger fish, and numerous alligator gar. Moki pointed out a hidden moray eel, and Jade brought an octopus from his hole in the sand. They saw sea turtles up close and personal, but a pod of dolphins only at a distance.

Still, Jade was happy to have a chance to educate them about all the various sea creatures, and she spoke at length. Amid much laughter, she even taught them to say *humuhumunukunukuapua'a*, the name of the Hawaiian state fish, an attractively marked triggerfish they saw over and over again.

Afterward, they rowed to a small cove where they beached the canoe, spread a towel and snacked on fruit and bottled drinks that they'd brought along in a cooler. Jade saw it as another opportunity to speak about sea life and the environment, even though she saw Moki rolling his eyes at her. He even pulled her aside at one point, speaking softly but urgently into her ear.

"Hey, what's with you this morning? You want to scare them away? Tone down, Professor. It's supposed to be fun."

Jade didn't let it bother her. She thought their guests were having a good time anyway. And they weren't too tired to help with the rowing again on the trip back.

Jade shook Warren's hand as he and Adam prepared to return to the hotel.

"It was nice meeting you, Warren. Will you be staying long?"

"Only a few more days."

"He's breaking up his trip from Japan to the Caribbean. Says he's getting too old to do the trip in one long haul."

Adam's voice indicated that he did not believe this to be true.

Jade laughed. "You are definitely too young to be feeling that way."

"That's very kind of you, my dear, but I know I'm an old man these days. Just look at this strapping lad that's my son."

His eyes traveled to Adam's tanned body, but Jade could see the pride he took in his son shining from his eyes.

"Anyway, that's only half the reason I stopped, and you know it."

His gently scolding tone made Adam wink at Jade, but Warren didn't see the irreverent gesture. Jade didn't have long to wonder what was going on between them.

Warren turned to Jade. "I stopped mainly to help him celebrate his birthday tomorrow. It's a biggie, his thirtieth."

Jade raised her brows as she focused on Adam, flashing him a teasing grin. "Thirty years old, huh?"

Adam shrugged. "It'll just be another working day. I have a meeting in Hilo."

Warren shook his head. "I may have taught the boy too well."

Jade noticed that he did not sound at all sorry about this. In fact, his eyes glowed with pride.

"But I'll be making him celebrate," Warren continued, "don't you worry. In fact, why don't you join us for dinner tomorrow night? It will be good for Adam to have a young person there. I'm suffering from jet lag, you know, so I don't know how long I'll last."

It was Adam's turn to raise his eyebrows. What was

his father doing? Setting him up with a date?

"I'm sure Jade has plans at this late date, Father."

Jade looked between the two of them. She liked them both. To her surprise, Warren acted like a "regular guy." If she hadn't known who he was, she'd have had no inkling that he was rich and important. And might control the future of her career.

She didn't have any plans for the following evening. Why not go to dinner with them?

"I don't have any plans, Adam. I'd love to help you celebrate your birthday."

Warren grinned. "Wonderful! You'll be good company for both Adam and Anne. Shall we pick you up, or would you prefer to meet us here?"

Jade laughed. "I don't think you'd want to drive all the way to Kona to pick me up when you're already here. Why don't I meet you? Just tell me when and where."

The arrangements were made with little regard to Adam or his opinion on the matter.

"See you tomorrow."

Jade waved to them both and hurried over to help Moki with the clean up.

Adam turned to his father. "You just railroaded that poor woman into coming to dinner with us tomorrow." Accusation laced his voice.

Warren seemed puzzled. "I thought you enjoyed her company and would like having her there. Was I wrong?"

Adam frowned. Of course he enjoyed Jade's company. Who wouldn't? She was pretty and pleasant and able to converse knowledgeably about many subjects. And she could kiss like a dream.

But he was a grown man. He could get his own dates.

Wasn't it enough that his father had chosen his career path? That his influence shadowed every aspect of his life?

Thirty years old and his father was still arranging birthday parties for him!

Jade spent the afternoon on basic household chores. Of course, such physical activities did not engage the mind, leaving it free to ponder her relationship with Adam. And to wonder about his father's impression of her.

As evening approached, she decided it was time to speak to her parents about the quilt.

Decision made, she lost no time heading over to her old home. Jade knew she would be welcome for dinner, even though she had not arranged it beforehand. Her father would be at his weekly tennis match with his friend Larry, and her mother would be puttering around the kitchen getting a meal ready for his return.

"Jade, sweetheart." Carol was delighted to see her oldest daughter, enveloping her in a bear hug. "You came for dinner, I hope."

"You don't mind, do you?"

"How can you even ask?"

Carol quickly had Jade settled at the kitchen table, an appetizer of fresh sliced mango before her.

Jade smiled at the sight of her mother moving around the kitchen. Much as she enjoyed the independence of her own place, she missed the friendly noises of a family, especially the sound and smells of her mother in the kitchen. Carol loved to cook and to bake, but Jade rarely had the time.

"There." Carol seated herself at the table, beside Jade. "Everything is just about done. We'll just wait for your father to get home."

She beamed at Jade. "So, tell me how you're doing."

"I love working at Dolphin Life Research."

Jade took another sliver of mango on her fork, biting delicately and savoring the sweetness against her tongue. When had she become such a sensuous person, so aware of flavors and scents?

It probably had something to do with a certain handsome *haole* gentleman who was celebrating a birthday tomorrow.

She swallowed the sweet fruit.

"Someone recently told me that I have a disgustingly happy smile on my face when I come in every morning. He called it unreal." She scrunched her nose up at the last, conveying her opinion of the comment.

Carol smiled. "He?"

"A guest at the hotel."

Jade laid her fork down on the table beside the fruit plate.

"Actually, he's more than a guest. He's looking into

140

buying the hotel for his father's company. Remember, I told you it's for sale? Everyone at Dolphin Life Research is worried about it."

"Do you think it will affect your jobs?"

Jade nodded. "It has to do with whether a new owner will want to try and persuade Dolphin Life Research to handle more swim with the dolphins sessions. We already do as much as we feel we can, keeping the health of the dolphins uppermost."

"I can see how that would concern you."

"I met his father this morning, while I was guiding a trek for Keoki. The CEO of Donovan Enterprises. I managed to do some sneaky lobbying while I educated them about the local sea life." She finished with a satisfied smile.

But there was something else bothering Jade at the moment—even more than the situation at Dolphin Life Research.

"Mom, when you gave me the quilt from Grandmother Helen, you said something about the *mana* being so strong it would help me find my true love."

Jade looked into her mother's serene face.

Carol nodded.

"How can I know if it's true love?"

Carol chuckled. "Ah, honey, if we knew the answer to that, we'd be rich." She thought for a moment. "I'd say it's just something you know in your heart. No one else can tell you. You have to listen to your heart, and trust it—that's the hardest part."

"Like thinking about someone twenty-four seven,

and wanting what's best for him? Wanting what will make him happy?"

Carol nodded again. "That can all be part of it."

Jade pushed the dish of fruit aside and folded her arms on the table in front of her.

"I met Adam the day after you gave me the quilt, Mom."

Carol's lips tightened, but quickly softened again. "I see. It has always worked quickly. But I did hope you would find someone here in the islands."

Jade shook her head. "But, Mom. Are you sure? This whole thing is so unreal. Not only the quilt, but Adam. Mom, he's an important international businessman. I can barely grasp the idea that he wants to spend time with me. Little me, from the Big Island."

"And what's wrong with that?" Carol's voice became defensive as it always did when someone implied one of her babies might not be perfect.

"You're a beautiful, intelligent woman with a lovely personality."

Jade smiled, then reached out to take and squeeze her mother's hand.

"Thank you, Mom, but you are a bit prejudiced."

Carol squeezed back before releasing her hand.

"Maybe, but you're still a lovely person."

"Tell me about the quilt, Mom. I've been having the strangest dreams, and I think it has something to do with the quilt."

Her father walked into the kitchen just in time to hear Jade's last sentence.

142

"Ah, so the quilt is working it's magic already, is it?"

Jade smiled. "Hi, Dad. How was the game?"

"Aw, I should have won."

Jade and Carol both smiled. Frank and his friend Larry were evenly matched opponents, and Frank inevitably grumbled when Larry won. Of course, Larry grumbled when Frank won.

Frank approached Carol, putting his arm around her and giving her a hello kiss along with the hug.

"You said it would work quickly. I don't know why I doubted you."

Jade frowned. They were back to the quilt.

"So you believe in it too? You don't think it's just a lot of superstitious nonsense?"

"On the contrary, Jade, I think the story of the Lovell quilt supports your mother's beliefs." Frank remained standing behind Carol's chair, his hand on her shoulder. "So do traditional Hawaiian beliefs. Your dreams, for instance. I think that has a lot to do with the *mana* in the quilt. Also with the Hawaiian belief that ancestors communicate with us through our dreams." He gave Jade a considering look. "Helen might be trying to tell you something."

Jade listened, her expression turning even more serious as she absorbed what her father was saying.

"Part of the *mana* in the quilt?"

He nodded, a big man with a proud face. "It was a powerful *mana*."

"Love always is," Carol agreed, reaching up to

grasp and squeeze the hand that still lay on her shoulder.

While Jade thought this over, Carol stood and began putting dinner on the table. Frank washed his hands at the sink and sat down. The three family members ate in comfortable silence in the old room. Used to the relative newness of her own condo, Jade noticed the faded paint of her mother's kitchen, the torn edge of one of the curtains. This was a room they used, a room they lived in. Not that any of the little defects mattered.

Jade had many happy memories of this old kitchen, especially the after school cookies and milk, along with conversations with her mother.

The silence had gone on for some time when Frank broke it. "I would be interested in hearing about your dreams, Jade."

Jade knew that her father was interested in all aspects of old Hawaiian lore. She supposed that to him the old quilt was a kind of research project.

Jade smiled. "Most of them have to do with dolphins."

Carol laughed. "Well, with you working with them all the time, I'm not surprised. You always have been crazy about dolphins."

"And they are the family *'aumakua,*" her father added.

Jade spoke of some of her dreams, explaining that she didn't always remember them clearly.

"Sometimes it's just a feeling I have when I wake up, and I know I was dreaming."

There was a long moment of silence after Jade finished speaking. Carol took the opportunity to bring everyone a cup of coffee. She set a plate of oatmeal cookies in the center of the table.

"Tell him about the man you've met," Carol urged. "Actually, tell us both. You haven't really said much about him."

So Jade told them about Adam.

"Do you think he's the one the quilt arranged for me to meet? That he's my true love?"

Jade heard herself speak the words and wondered if she'd gone nuts. But something strange was going on, and she wanted to explore the possibilities. Before she joined Adam and his family at dinner tomorrow.

"Oh, we can't tell you that, honey. There's no way for us to know." Carol patted her hand. "Like I told you, you'll have to decide for yourself."

"Has the quilt always been right?"

Carol didn't answer, just smiled.

"Your mother is the one who formulated this theory about the quilt," Frank said, "and how through it Helen helps her descendants find true love. Tell her how you did it, hon."

"My mother, your Grandma Lucas, gave me the quilt when I finished nursing school. I met your Dad right away, and we were married six months later. After your Dad and I got married, I put the quilt on our bed. We slept under it for the first year." She smiled at Jade. "You know, honey, I had some interesting dreams then too. I'd forgotten all about that."

Carol continued to talk about the women of their family, about their courtships and their success in choosing men as lifetime partners.

By the time Jade left for home, long after dark, she was more confused than ever.

Adam awoke early on the morning of his birthday. He had a luncheon meeting with representatives of the Hawaii Visitor's Bureau and some county officials about the present state of tourism on the island and future projections. He'd wanted to keep busy on this of all days. He'd invited Warren to accompany him, but his father had Anne to meet at the airport.

Seeing the gloomy skies outside the window, Adam had a brief moment of regret. He could have had the day off and slept in this drizzly morning. Instead, he'd wanted to pretend it was just another workday, so now he had to follow through.

Warren found Adam standing before the sliding glass doors of the suite's living room, looking out at a gray sky that blended into a gray ocean.

"Hard to tell where the ocean ends and the sky begins."

Adam started. He'd been deep in thought, staring out at the dismal day but not really seeing it.

"Good morning, Father. You're up early."

Warren's left eyebrow rose. "I was thinking the same of you."

That brought a shrug. "I've gotten into the habit of rising early. You get a lot done when you get an early start. So what's your excuse?"

Warren grinned. "The same, actually. Bet you didn't realize how much you have in common with your old man."

Adam was caught by surprise. Was he really so much like his father? A few days ago the thought might have brought a quick denial. Today, a surge of pride flooded his chest.

The corners of his mouth were nudging upward when Adam finally turned from the patio doors to see Warren approaching with two mugs of coffee.

"I started the coffeemaker when I got up. Nothing like a good jolt of caffeine to start the day."

Adam accepted a cup with thanks.

But despite his comment, Warren continued to hold his cup, not raising it to his lips. His expression was serious as he focused on his son.

"You've turned into a fine young man, Adam. A man I'm proud of. I guess I don't tell you often enough. You're a fine addition to the company, and I'm proud to call you my son."

Adam blinked as he felt an unaccustomed burning sensation in his eyes. He cleared his throat. "Thank you, Father."

Warren glanced down into his mug, speaking in a manner that Adam read as embarrassed.

"I have to admit, I didn't always think you'd do me so proud, son. There was a time there when you seemed determined to pursue *plants* as a career."

Warren seemed to hear his words and realize they were not what he'd hoped to say. Scorn laced his voice, giving the word an emphasis he had not intended. He stumbled over the next sentence, hurrying to get the words out. "Not that I'd ever be ashamed of you. That's not what I meant."

"I know what you meant."

Adam knew that Warren had always considered his interest in plants "unmanly." Maybe because of his interest in hybrid flowers. Warren would have felt respect for a son with an advanced scientific degree, especially one who accomplished something with his work. But a son who followed him into his company, the company he'd devoted his life to—that was a son he could really be proud of. His mother had been right.

Warren was still trying to explain himself. "I'd have been proud, whatever you did. I'm sure you would be successful in any field, because you're a dedicated and hard worker. But there's something very special about having your son follow in your footsteps."

Adam nodded. His father was trying to tell him that he appreciated him and the work he did. It was his idea of a birthday present.

"I've often wondered if I should have pursued a career in botany." Adam noticed a furrow appear on Warren's forehead. "But I know how special it is to work in a family business."

He was pleased to see his father's features relax, his mouth soften, ready to smile.

"Growing things is a good hobby, one I can enjoy for the rest of my life."

Warren was smiling now, though his eyes appeared watery. He clapped his son on the back.

"This is a very special day, Adam."

"I agree."

Adam put one arm around his father. So what if they never hugged? One time was all he needed.

Warren seemed surprised, but returned the one-armed hug. Then the two men sprang apart, retreating to their rooms, coffee mugs still in hand. This new level of emotional involvement would take some getting used to, Adam thought, as he finally sampled the coffee.

Adam put aside the mug with a grimace. Warren made the worst coffee in the world!

As Adam prepared to leave sometime later, he paused at the wide glass doors. A gloomy drizzle continued to fall, the gray skies toning down the usually spectacular view.

What was Jade's frame of mind on this gray day?

Determined to find out before he left for Hilo—and to ascertain whether she really wanted to attend his birthday dinner or had simply felt coerced into coming—Adam headed for the dolphin lagoon.

Despite the gloomy skies, it was business as usual at Dolphin Life Research. Less people might wander by the dolphin lagoon, but lottery winners were sure to appear, and school classes would follow through on arrangements made long ago.

Adam could pick out Jade's petite figure as soon as

he stepped from the building leading toward the dolphin pool. She sat on the low wooden deck that floated above the water of the man-made lagoon, writing on a clipboard. He made no noise as he stepped up to the wooden railing, yet she turned immediately and looked into his eyes.

Déjà vu, Adam thought, reminded of that first evening when he'd seen her at the reception. The impact of that first meeting of their eyes was just as devastating now as it had been then.

"Well, hello."

Her quietly voiced words were just audible over the washing of the ocean's waves on the rocky, true beach some hundred feet away. She sounded breathless, and Adam hoped it was because his presence was as special to her as seeing her was to him.

She looked beautiful. In deference to the drizzle, she wore a sweatshirt over her swimsuit. But her long legs were bare beneath the gray-ribbed hem and her feet were slippered in the rubber thongs worn by so many islanders.

He smiled. "I was wondering if you tripped up the walkway with a smile on your face this morning."

"Well, of course."

But her teasing smile had Adam guessing at the truth—that she had dragged a bit on this rainy morning. And why not? The residents of West Hawaii were spoiled by their usually perfect weather. The sunshine was one of the reasons the area was such a popular resort location.

Adam nodded but didn't smile. His expression remained serious as he examined her face. "Jade. My father put you in an awkward position yesterday. You don't have to come tonight unless you really want to."

A myriad of emotions passed over Jade's countenance before she replied. Adam could see that she was alternately surprised, resigned, disappointed, hurt . . .

Damn. He hadn't meant to hurt her.

"I don't have to come if you don't want me to."

Adam frowned. "Now I've gone and done it. I didn't want you to feel pressured into accepting an invitation you didn't want. But I've managed to make you feel unwelcome instead."

Adam squatted down on his haunches to bring himself closer to her eye level. "Jade, I would love to have you help celebrate my birthday. As long as you want to be there. In fact, I can't think of anything I'd like more."

Jade smiled—a wide, happy smile. Adam felt its effects deep inside his chest, where warmth radiated outward from his heart. As though the whole earth agreed that it was turning into a lovely day after all, the clouds parted and a ray of sunshine brightened the dolphin lagoon. The drizzle had turned into a fine mist, barely felt, and along with the newly discovered sun, it produced a rainbow. Adam dimly heard guests exclaiming over the weather phenomenon that he knew was quite common in the islands.

He didn't drag his eyes from Jade until he saw her looking up at the colorful arc. It stretched *mauka* to *makai,* from the green mountain far inland, its summit still shrouded in clouds, to the choppy gray seas.

He heard Jade's rapid intake of breath just as his eyes saw the movement at the end of the rainbow. Fish were leaping from the sea, playing joyfully in the warm waters of the Pacific. Not fish, he realized. Dolphins.

"The treasure at the end of the rainbow."

Jade spoke softly, a touch of pure delight evident on her face. Adam doubted that any of the nearby guests exclaiming over the rainbow heard her. Did any of the others, less attuned to dolphins than Jade, even see the playful mammals frolicking?

But he heard her, and he felt a smile soften his lips. He hadn't believed Jade when she said she'd headed for work this morning with her usual high spirits. He didn't doubt that she loved her job, just as she claimed. But earlier, there just hadn't been the usual elation in her expression. Now, she was back to her old self, her eyes sparkling, happiness radiating not only from her face but from her whole body.

The rainbow faded as a cloud covered the sun. It was a signal for Adam to return to their interrupted conversation.

"I'd like to have you join me for dinner," he assured her.

"In that case, I'd like to come."

Jade stood on the low deck, just above the water of the lagoon, ignoring the dolphins swimming just a few feet away. With Adam squatting, they were at eye level.

"Do you know where we'll be going? So I know what to wear," she hastened to add.

Her question was a rude reality check, a brutal reminder of past relationships. "Where will we be dining, Adam? You know how I love to dress up." He'd eventually learned this was really a thinly disguised request for him to spend as much as possible on his date—to take her to expensive places where she could be seen by important people.

He'd like to see Jade's reaction if he said they would be driving over to MacDonald's. But he couldn't, as Warren had issued the invitation. And knowing his father, he would have made reservations at just the sort of place his former girlfriend preferred.

"Knowing Dad, he's made reservations at one of the best restaurants in the hotel. Probably the steakhouse. So dress up. But whatever you wear, I'm sure I'll be the envy of every man in the place."

He was delighted to see the blush that colored Jade's cheeks. He was right about her, definitely old-fashioned. And he found that he liked it. He'd dated any number of modern, sophisticated women over the years, without finding anyone he wanted to be with for more than a short time.

Perhaps all along he'd been looking for the wrong kind of woman. Because now he could imagine a long-term relationship with a woman as sweet and as fascinating as Jade Kanahele.

• • •

Dinner was almost over, and Jade couldn't recall when she'd had such a good time. She caught herself just before she referred to the evening as a date. This wasn't a date. She'd been asked to fill in, to make a fourth, so that Adam's dinner party would be more even. To be the young guest who could share contemporary interests with Adam.

She was glad she'd been asked. She always enjoyed her time with Adam, and Warren and Anne were also good company. Any lingering fears she'd had about how she might be treated were rapidly banished. They seemed to like her company as much as she liked theirs.

And being there had nothing to do with falling in love or Grandmother Helen's quilt. As she'd told Tami and Ryan that afternoon, it was a prime opportunity to further her lobbying efforts with the Donovan Enterprises' CEO.

The evening began when Adam, Warren, and Anne met her in the lobby at the designated time. As soon as she and Anne were introduced, Jade presented Adam with a wrapped gift. He'd protested heavily, claiming not to expect a gift from her, then scolding her for going to the expense, not to mention the trouble of wrapping it so beautifully.

She had worked hard to make the wrapping pretty and was unaccountably tickled that he'd noticed. She'd used a sea green paper with a wave-like pattern, then mixed several shades of blue and green curling ribbon to make a large puffy bow overflowing with curls.

The confident young businessman disappeared, momentarily replaced by a grinning boy asking if he could open it immediately.

Warren protested. "Show a little restraint boy. If you do it here, we'll be late to claim our table. Come along, you can open it once we're seated in the restaurant."

As Adam had suspected, they proceeded to the hotel's steakhouse, a four-star restaurant written up in all the guidebooks. Jade had never eaten there, felt intimidated just walking in the door. She'd heard about the prices, and knew the rumors were justified when she received a menu to peruse that had none.

But Adam's suggestion that she dress up at least had her feeling good about her appearance. She'd chosen that perennial favorite, a slim black dress. She'd dressed it up with a gold chain holding a golden dolphin pendant, and her gold Hawaiian heritage bracelet with her name etched in black. Looking around her at the other patrons, she felt comfortable and was able to relax while Adam tore into his gift.

"Jade. It's beautiful. And much too expensive a gift."

Adam looked from Jade to the small watercolor in his hands, and back to Jade. "This is wonderful. But I can't allow you to spend so much." Warren and Anne added their admiration of the piece.

Jade laughed. She could see it surprised him, which only made her laugh more.

"My cousin Chrissie will be delighted to hear it. She paints these for a little gallery in Kona, and she does okay. But they don't cost as much as you seem to think. And I got the family discount," she added with a saucy grin.

Adam glanced again at the painting. Jade had chosen it particularly for him. It showed a pair of dolphins leaping from the ocean, a rainbow in the sky above. The colors were bright and sharp, the execution perfect. Yesterday, when she chose it, she couldn't have known exactly how singular it would be.

"It's a very special gift, Jade. Thank you."

He put it back into the box she'd used to wrap it, then stored it protectively under the table.

The watercolor proved a perfect way to introduce the topic of dolphins and Dolphin Life Research. Jade was able to offer her opinions in a way she thought provided the proper information without being pedantic or preachy. Or obvious.

Now, as they finished their meals, Warren pulled his birthday gift from an inner pocket.

"I'm sure this will pale after the lovely painting from Jade, but I didn't want to let your birthday pass without a little something." He handed the small, somberly wrapped package to Adam.

Adam thanked his father as he pulled the paper from the latest PDA. He thanked him, laughing about how much more efficient he could be, business-wise, with his new gadget. Then he protested once more as Anne removed a small package from her purse.

"You shouldn't have, Anne."

But she pushed aside his objections.

"It's just not a proper birthday without gifts."

Jade agreed.

Anne's gift was a slim book of exquisitely done botanical drawings. He raised his eyes to meet her gaze, and Jade could see that he was awed by how perfect her choice was.

"Thank you, Anne. I can't tell you how much this means to me."

Jade knew he meant it. It wasn't just the book itself that pleased him. It was Anne's knowledge that it would be special to him.

Chapter Nine

Unlike Jade's body temperature, the evening air was cool when Adam and Jade left the restaurant. Adam had his hand on the small of Jade's back to guide her, and the physical link kept his heart beating at a high rate. Her internal thermostat must be set on high because heat flowed from her, warming him as well.

Warren and Anne decided to drop in at the bar to take in the floor show. "It's my first time in Hawaii," Anne said, apologizing for breaking up the party. "I'd love to hear some traditional music."

Jade chimed in on the side of ending the evening. "I have to work in the morning," she reminded them.

Now she walked beside Adam as they headed for the employee parking lot. Not that Adam's guidance was necessary. She knew the way better than he did. And he was sure the path wasn't dangerous. But she brought out all his latent protective urges, making him feel that she should be able to do more than merely walk her to her car.

"Shall I take you home?"

Adam could see that his question caught Jade unaware. And why not? He'd surprised himself with the suggestion. But anything that would prolong his time with Jade sounded good at the moment.

"Take me home?" Jade repeated.

The idea sounded better and better to Adam. "Why not? I could drive you home. I have a rental car."

Jade laughed. "It's very gallant of you to offer. But how would I get to work in the morning?"

Adam grinned. "You could offer me breakfast."

Jade responded with an exaggerated moue of shock. She was apparently holding with the light, jesting mood they had maintained throughout the evening.

"Or," he continued, "you could stay the night here. That way neither of us would have to drive all the way to Kona in the dark, and you'd be on the premises in the morning."

"In my best dress," Jade reminded him.

"Hmm. I had a feeling there might be a problem with that." His voice turned soft, sensuous. "But you have to admit it was a great idea."

He turned toward her, stopping them in a quiet corner of the side lobby. Where they stood, the lobby's bright lights were muted, cast toward artwork in a glass case against the wall. Adam could see the smooth planes of Jade's lovely features, seeming harsh in the purple shadows. But one thing Adam knew for certain about Jade Kanahele—she would never be harsh. She had a soft heart—for all of God's creatures.

"Good ideas aren't always the best ideas."

Adam's smile was gone; his eyes burned into Jade's. He wanted nothing more than to feel his lips meet hers. The memory of their earlier kisses filled him.

Whether suddenly shy or frightened by his intensity, Jade shuttered her eyes.

Adam pulled her into his arms.

But she was restless, and her body fidgeted as nervously as her gaze.

And she was going to kill him with those little uneasy movements. But they did tell him she wasn't ready for another kiss. Yet releasing her was almost more than he could handle. Adam pressed a quick, firm kiss on her moistened lips then reluctantly released her, stepping back at the same time to put some distance between them. He needed that space, or he'd pull her back into his arms and kiss her until neither of them knew where they were. Or cared.

But he was forced to immediately reach for Jade's arm again, as she stumbled and almost fell.

So he wasn't the only one feeling that pull between them. He'd asked her to stay the night in a jesting mood, though he'd known she would not.

He watched silently as she pulled herself together.

They both needed a moment to stabilize their runaway feelings. But he felt better knowing he wasn't alone with his extreme reactions to her.

Adam put his arm around Jade's shoulders.

"Let's go look at the fountain." Beyond the shadowed lobby where they stood, bright lights illuminated a courtyard fountain. The trickling of the water offered a soothing, cooling appeal.

Adam guided Jade outside until they stood before the fountain, a huge concrete affair with sculpted brass tropical maidens holding baskets and gourds in their arms. The water gushed from a high, central rock-like well into their gourds and baskets, flowing from one to another among the standing and sitting maidens.

Adam and Jade stood quietly beside the large structure, admiring the sculpted figures. A cool breeze touched their skin and guitar music drifted on the night air. Adam worked at busying his mind with something other than the warm presence of Jade beside him. The sensuous music did not help, having the exact opposite effect. So did the light, outdoorsy perfume she wore, which tickled his senses with every small move she made.

Then an idea penetrated the desire clouding his brain. He released Jade to reach into his pocket for some change.

"Want to make a wish?"

Jade eagerly assented.

Together they threw their respective coins into the water. Jade's fell into the large main pool, but Adam's flew high, arcing over the pool before dropping with a soft plop into the wide low basket of a sitting maiden. Jade watched his coin with interest, squealing with delight when it landed in the basket of the bronze maiden.

"Great throw."

They continued to stand, arms around each other, listening to the susurration of the water.

"Hmmm."

Jade's soft murmur shivered into his consciousness.

"You got two wishes tonight—one on your birthday cake candle, and one now." Warren had seen to it that a small cake was provided after their meal, and it had arrived trimmed with a fat candle that Adam promptly blew out.

"Ah, but I made the same wish."

Jade looked up at him through her lashes, a mannerism that filled Adam with desire.

"What was it?"

Adam clicked his tongue. "You know I can't tell. The wish doesn't come true if you tell."

"Hmm."

Adam pulled back enough to look down into her face. "What do you mean 'hmm.' That's a well-known, universal fact."

"Oh, I know that. It just strikes me as odd that a big guy like you should still believe in birthday wishes." She nestled closer against him, no longer feeling too warm, just enjoying the contact. "I think it's nice actually."

"Nice." Adam shook his head slowly. "The kiss of death as far as a guy is concerned."

Jade snuggled closer. "I don't know why. Nice is a good word. It means a person cares about other people. Doesn't just want what's best for himself. It's a good thing to say about a guy."

"If you say so. But you're going to ruin my reputation as a hard-hitting, ruthless businessman."

Jade cricked her neck up to see his face. Bad mistake. He was looking down on her, his eyes tender, but burning with—what? Desire? Admiration? Jade wasn't sure, and she wasn't sure she wanted to know.

"I guess I should be going."

But she made no attempt to step away from him. She remained where she was, his arm around her shoulder, her arm around his waist. It was a comfortable position. So comfortable it almost scared her.

"I guess you should."

But he made no attempt to move either. Together, they remained there beside the fountain, breathing in the fragrant perfume of a tropical night. The clouds of the morning well and truly gone, masses of stars twinkled overhead. Even with the lighting on the hotel grounds, the abundance of stars was evident. In the background, the sound of the ocean waves could be heard. The soothing guitar music was gone, replaced by the throbbing, primal beat of Tahitian drums.

It was time to get moving.

"Are you parked in the lot on the other side of the gardens again?"

"Uh-huh."

"I'll walk you out. You shouldn't go all that way alone in the dark."

Jade was thrilled by Adam's concern, but she had to respond to his insinuation that the path might not be safe.

"It's not dangerous walking on the hotel grounds, Adam."

Adam blinked, as though just becoming aware of that aspect of his remark.

"Of course. I didn't mean that it was. I just don't want you to have to walk all that way alone. The least I can do is see my date to her car, since I can't drive her home."

Was this a date after all then? Jade wondered. A thrill of pleasure heavily mixed with apprehension passed through her. If she'd ever doubted it, being with Adam and his father tonight confirmed his privileged background. Warren's reminiscences told of a child who had everything he wanted growing up. How could she ever hope to fit into his life?

The dinner with Adam and his family had been the best evening she'd had in too long. She needed to get out again, start reestablishing friendships that had faltered while she spent so much time earning her degree. She knew that some of her girlhood friends were still in the area. Eating out with these new friends had been so much fun, she should get out more often. Perhaps then she would not have those strange dreams that left her unsettled and lonely.

Most important, she'd felt comfortable with Adam, Warren, and Anne. Maybe *too* comfortable with Adam. Her doubts about his family's reaction to her allayed, she still could not banish the thought of Teddy's snobbish parents looking down on her.

And she needed to banish those unwelcome thoughts. It was a beautiful night, and she'd just finished a delicious dinner. And she had the best-looking man at the resort standing at her side.

Jade smiled, thinking of her fountain wish—that she could decide exactly what the relationship was between herself and her handsome escort.

"You are a nice man, Adam."

He groaned.

Jade shivered. The sound was too much like the one he'd uttered earlier, when he'd had his arms around her. His jesting request that she spend the night had been much too appealing. She couldn't let him know how tempted she was! That was why she'd been so anxious to break from his embrace.

"Are you cold?"

"No. Well, maybe a little. We should start walking again."

They took a last lingering look at the water spilling from gourd to basket, then turned and headed for the parking lot.

The gardens were as lovely at night as they were during the day. Lit by moonlight and starlight, and by soft, low lights that ran along the pathways, the plants almost glowed. The white blossoms especially—the tiare, gardenias, plumeria—shone like the finest pearls. Their perfume mixed together into a light, heady fragrance that permeated the garden, and beyond.

Jade and Adam maintained a slow pace. Although she knew she must go, she was reluctant to end this time with Adam.

The evening was taking on a definite dreamlike quality. Jade tried not to notice the romantic atmosphere created by the soft lighting and the twinkling stars. As they moved away from the main buildings, more and more stars became visible.

Their arms still around each other, Jade's and Adam's footsteps slowed. The air seemed thicker out here, heavy with damp and salt. The scent of the ocean filled Jade's nostrils—the scent of home. She thought she could hear dolphins calling out, wondered that their clicks and whistles could be heard so far from the lagoon.

A feeling of languor filled her, and a pleasant warmth suffused her body. She felt as though she was curled up under her quilt at home, trying to pull herself from one of the quilt-induced dreams.

"Penny for your thoughts."

Adam's softly spoken words caused Jade to start with surprise. She was so aware of her own body, of her surroundings, of the scents and sounds of the night, she'd almost forgotten he was there. Which didn't make any sense at all, since his presence was the catalyst that had caused the sensation that made her feel so lethargic.

Jade squeezed Adam's waist, distracting herself for a moment with the feel of him. He felt so good beneath her arm.

"You'd be wasting your money, Adam. I wasn't actually thinking, just feeling."

Adam choked. Jade couldn't imagine how as he had not been eating anything, but he coughed heavily, pulling away from her as he bent over at the waist, trying to clear his throat.

Feeling helpless, Jade pounded on his back. She didn't know if it helped, but she had to do something.

Finally, Adam straightened, cleared his throat, and took Jade's hand. "It's okay. I'm okay. Just swallowed wrong."

Jade covered their hands with her other. "Are you sure? Maybe we should get you some water." She glanced back at the hotel buildings. The ones near them were guest rooms. The nearest public area was several minutes away.

"Thanks, but I'm fine."

They resumed their trip to the parking lot. Jade felt that the distance had increased tremendously since she'd parked there earlier. Finally, she saw the *'ohi'a lehua* hedge that marked the perimeter of the parking lot.

"What were you feeling?"

Adam's voice was low, just loud enough for her to hear. The words seemed to be pulled from him, as though, he was reluctant to speak them but had to.

Jade halted, turned.

"I was feeling the night." Her voice too was pitched low, as though speaking out would break some fragile contact with the magic she felt.

"The night?"

"The night," she repeated. "The air, the humidity, the warmth of it. It's cooler than in the daytime when the sun is out of course, but it's still more warm than not at this time of year. And I was noticing the scent of the ocean, hearing the waves and the sounds of the dolphins over in their lagoon. And I could smell the flowers, the perfume of different tropical blossoms floating in the night air."

Jade moved slightly as she spoke and shivered when she felt Adam's breath feather across her forehead.

"I've been to the mainland, and that's the first thing I notice when I return to Hawaii. The air here has a unique scent. It has to be the blooming tropical plants, because it's a perfumed kind of smell, and I've never noticed anything remotely like it on the mainland."

Adam's head nodded slowly. Or was he just leaning toward her? Bringing his head closer, within kissing distance?

Suddenly all Jade could think about was another kiss. Would he?

Adam brushed her lips with his. It was so light, so gentle, she wondered if she'd wished it into existence. But, no, it had to have been real. Her lips tingled with it, and now he had moved his lips to her cheek, heading toward her ear, raining light kisses all along the way.

Jade wondered if her toes were curling up in her open-toed dressy sandals. She wouldn't be surprised if they were. Her arms wound around Adam, smoothing up his back.

But enough of this. She angled her lips toward his. The light, butterfly kisses he was trailing across her cheek were wonderful, sending tickles of sensation rippling through her body. How had she ever managed to meet such a nice man, a man who could make her feel so much with just one kiss? She needed him.

Startled by the deep need she felt, Jade quickly pulled back, surprising herself almost as much as she surprised Adam. For a moment, she thought he meant to pull her back against him.

"What is it?" His voice rasped from his throat.

Adam reached for her again, a dazed look of confusion on his face. He didn't seem ready to stop their good-bye kisses, but she had to. Now.

"I, ah, have to go. Work tomorrow."

She twisted from his grip, stepping between the hedge and toward the row of cars where she had parked. Then she stopped and turned back, almost slamming against Adam who was right behind her. She almost jumped backward, but was stopped by his hands reaching out to steady her. She rested in his arms for a moment, trying to prolong the magic of the evening.

Then she tipped her head up to look into his face. "Thank you for letting me share your birthday with you, Adam."

Adam remained silent for a moment. When he spoke, his voice was the familiar, polite one.

"It was my pleasure." He stepped up beside her. "I'll escort you to your car."

She knew better than to try to dissuade him. Together they walked the few feet in silence. At the car, he took the keys from her hand and unlocked her door. But he stopped her before she could climb into the driver's seat.

"Good night, Jade."

For one final time, he pulled her into his arms and kissed her good night. Jade wished he never had to let her go.

Jade lay in bed staring at the ceiling for a long time before falling asleep. She could not forget those last kisses she'd shared with Adam, the one in the garden and the final one as they stood beside her car. The feelings that roared through her almost defied identification, so varied and numerous were they.

In the summer, Jade slept with the blinds and windows open. A bright moon cast silvery shadows in the room, and her eyes strayed to her special quilt. Folded back, the light dim, it appeared as a series of floral shadows.

Jade recalled her Grandma Lucas telling her that no one knew where Hawaiian-style quilts had originated. One of the stories told of a woman who spread her sheets to dry under an *ulu* tree and saw the shadow thrown by the sun upon her white sheets. She then proceeded to cut and sew the first Hawaiian quilt, an *ulu* design. It was the pattern suggested as a starting place for aspiring quilters.

Tonight, in the grayness of her bedroom, Jade could truly imagine that as the beginnings of the art. The red fabric of the quilt looked dark gray in the moonshine, while the white background almost glowed with a silver sheen. Hina, as though knowing she should not lie on the old quilt, was curled into a ball on the sheet, pressing against Jade's sheet-covered legs on one side and the folded edge of the quilt on the other. Jade noticed that *she* wasn't having any problems dropping off to sleep.

Propped up on her pillows, examining the intricacies of her ancestor's quilt, Jade finally fell into a restless sleep.

Dreams troubled her, so that she did not feel rested when her alarm sounded the following morning. She flung out her arm to turn off the ringing, then pushed the sheet away. The night must have grown cold, as not only the sheet was pulled up over her body, but the antique quilt as well.

"Oh, dear," Jade murmured, unaware she spoke the words aloud. "I've got to be more careful of that quilt."

She straightened the bed, smoothing the old quilt gently, probing at folds to be sure it was all right. Hina uncurled herself from the pillow where she had been fast asleep and stretched languorously. She then approached her mistress with an indignant meow, rather for waking her or in requesting her breakfast Jade couldn't be sure. She was too busy to worry about it, her fingers moving lightly over a red blossom checking for any damage.

"I hope you didn't sleep on it," she told Hina.

As though she understood every word, Hina answered with an indignant meow.

Jade was petting Hina and assuring her that she trusted her completely, when she remembered a dream.

She'd been swimming in the ocean, swimming with a pod of wild dolphins. Jade had done this during her internship, spent time with a researcher in Kealakekua who worked with wild spinner dolphins. It was exciting, swimming with numerous animals in the ocean, a totally different experience than working with the few they had in the hotel's lagoon.

In the dream, Jade remembered, she'd been swimming peacefully, experiencing the tranquility and joy that came with interacting with her personal *'aumakua*. The feeling of being one with them was so special, it made her heart sing, made her feel that she had reached a pinnacle of success in life.

Then suddenly, the serenity was gone. Lost.

The water turned from aqua to white. It churned, swelled, sucked her into its depths. She floundered, struggling to keep afloat.

And none of the dolphins came to her aid as that one had done so long ago.

As the terror of her dream swamped her once again,

Jade realized why her sleep had not been restful. How could it have been with this experience, even now, so real?

She pulled Hina into her arms, hugging her so close the cat meowed a protest. With soft murmurings of apology, Jade released the poor animal. Thankfully, she realized that her mistress needed her, and stayed at her side, rubbing her soft head against Jade's arm.

Jade touched her head lightly, then scratched her ears, just at the base near the center of her head where she liked it best. Hina purred loudly, delighted with Jade's actions. She stepped delicately into Jade's lap, curled into a furry gray ball and closed her eyes.

Jade shook her head at the cat, but was grateful for her comforting presence. The emptiness she'd felt in her dream still haunted her, leaving her feeling empty inside. Barren.

What could it mean?

She stared at the quilt that she'd slept beneath, unaware of its presence over her. If her mother was to be believed, the quilt had so much *mana,* it could help the women of the family find their true loves. Helen had visited her husband's dreams whenever he'd used the quilt. But there hadn't been a woman in Jade's dream. So what exactly was her ancestor trying to tell her?

Jade gazed at the walls of her bedroom. With time and money scarce, she hadn't had a chance to decorate the way she hoped to, so the walls were still bare. Barren.

Did that have something to do with the dream? Was Grandmother Helen trying to tell her that her life was barren? Did the white water, bleached of its beautiful azure tint, symbolize the sterile white walls of her new home?

Perhaps she should she paint the bedroom—a pale azure blue sounded like a soothing color. Though it wouldn't exactly match Helen's quilt.

Then there was the churning water, the undertow that pulled her down. Could that have something to do with her relationship with Adam? Was it even a relationship?

Jade continued to scratch Hina's ears. The cat purred, pushing herself more deeply into Jade's lap. The warm animal heat spread through her, but it had little in common with the heat that came with Adam's touch.

Adam. Just thinking his name brought a spark of pleasure that raced through her, increasing her heartbeat and warming her cheeks.

Jade's hands flew to her cheeks, one palm covering each warm curve of flesh. Her mother and father, even Momi seemed to believe in the quilt. Could they be right? Had the quilt coming into her possession caused her to meet Adam? Caused them to fall in love? Because she thought that it was love—on her side at least. She couldn't know about Adam's side.

The whole idea was so outrageous. Yet. . . . Yet. . . .

Jade thought back to their meeting, the way she hadn't been able to get him out of her mind. How thoughts of him haunted her first day at work, pictures of him so detailed there was no way she could have actually seen and remembered them.

And comments Adam made led her to believe that he had had a similar reaction.

Still, it was too far-fetched.

Jade's hands fell back into her lap and her eyes rounded. Just as far-fetched as an ancestor represented by a dolphin who came to her rescue when she might have drowned. Or who visited her dreams.

Jade swallowed. Perhaps the dream was merely a reflection of her state of mind. She was drowning in confusion.

One thing she was no longer confused about, however. She, Jade Kanahele, was a worthy individual with a stellar ancestral background. She wasn't going to let anyone put her down again for being who she was.

She dressed slowly that morning, and skipped breakfast. Her stomach was tied up in knots as her mind spun with new ideas. New concepts. As she started her car, she hoped that a busy day of school visits was scheduled for her. She'd need the distraction to get through this day.

The distraction she got was not what she'd had in mind. It came in the person of Adam Donovan, dressed in swim trunks and a T-shirt, reporting for the morning swim with the dolphins session. Jade saw him and grabbed the roster from Tami's hands, her eyes quickly scanning the names.

"Oh, dear."

Tami raised her carefully plucked eyebrows.

"I thought you and Mr. Donovan were the best of friends. Have a fight, did you?"

The tone was teasing but the insinuation was obvious.

Jade could feel the heat rush to her cheeks and wished there was some way to control the involuntary reaction. She was doing altogether too much blushing these days. A woman her age should be past all that.

"We are friends. I just don't think I want him here while I'm working. Think about it. He must be checking us out, seeing what we do, how he could add to it. And I thought I did so well last night too."

"Hasn't he said anything about his plans yet?"

Jade shook her head. "He doesn't talk much about himself, and even less about business."

With a frown, Tami moved away to begin greeting their guests. Jade noted, however, that Tami quickly flashed a smile as she approached Adam. A particularly warm smile. The sight of it made Jade's stomach churn with jealousy. Tami was so pretty. And her tall tanned body complimented Adam's. They made a great-looking couple.

Jade felt a pang in her chest, and she found herself searching Adam's face, trying to interpret his response to the other woman. He'd been very nice to her ever since they met, but was that the way he treated everyone? He didn't kiss everyone he met, did he? He'd kissed her like no one ever had before.

The question was: did he love her? Because she had fallen head over heels for Adam, probably the first time she saw him. And it took an attack of jealousy to make her certain of it.

Schooling her features into what she sincerely hoped was a pleasant expression, Jade walked over to Adam.

"Hello."

The smile that transformed his face gave her hope.

"Hello yourself. You're looking terrific this morning."

"Not too happy?"

The question made his eyes sparkle with mischief, and Jade felt her heart melt.

While Jade enjoyed teaching Adam about the dolphins, getting to introduce him to them in a more personal way, his presence made the entire session stressful. She was so aware of Adam physically, it was a constant battle to keep her mind on track. She didn't want to explain about the eating habits of dolphins, she just wanted to get closer to Adam.

But the hour was eventually up and the participants drifted off, anxious to tell their families about their experience.

All except Adam. He stayed near Jade as she worked with the others to clean up.

"Will you be getting off for lunch now?"

"When I'm finished here. It will be a few more minutes."

She had to step around him to replace the life vests. "Especially if you keep getting in my way."

"Sorry."

He didn't look sorry. In fact, he seemed smugly satisfied about something. But he did scoop up the last two vests and hand them to her. "Have lunch with me. We could go to the golf club again. I enjoyed the view there, and the food was good."

Jade felt herself melting. Again. No matter how much he disliked the word, he was such a nice man. He obviously recalled her preference not to eat at the Thatched Hut the previous week, offering her an alternative.

But it was his next softly voiced words that tipped the balance. He leaned in close, so close his breath fanned her ear.

"And the company was unsurpassed."

Jade could feel warmth flood her.

"I'd love to join you for lunch."

Behind Adam, Jade saw Tami wink.

She frowned. Not at Tami, but at herself for succumbing so easily to Adam's charm. But when he smiled at her that way . . .

Chapter Ten

"It was nice seeing you again, Father."

Adam had driven his father and Anne to the airport. Warren and Anne planned to enjoy a few days on Maui before heading back to Florida and the Caribbean. Bags checked, tickets ready, they stood together at the security checkpoint saying their good-byes.

"I'm glad you decided to stop off in Hawaii," Adam continued. "It's been a long time since you helped me celebrate a birthday. It made me feel young again," he added. "Especially when you invited a date for me."

Warren had the grace to look embarrassed. "I thought you'd enjoy having someone your own age."

Adam clapped him on the back. "I did." He decided not to go into the reason he'd initially objected. "Having you here made this birthday special."

"Thank you, son. But I think it might have been Jade who made it special. She's quite a woman, Adam."

Adam had to agree.

Warren placed his hand on his son's shoulder. "We don't see enough of each other anymore, son. We should make more of an effort." He sighed. "*I* should make more of an effort. But it is difficult when we're often working on opposite sides of the world."

Adam smiled at Anne. "And now you'll be too busy for me, I'm sure. But I expect an invitation to the wedding. I want a chance to kiss the bride."

"You can kiss me anytime, Adam."

Anne's cheeks turned a light pink at her bold words, and Adam's lips twitched as he tried not to laugh. He leaned over instead and placed a chaste kiss on her cheek. And thought again how lucky his father was to have found another wonderful woman.

"I'll be in touch." Warren put his arm around Anne, looking down at her tenderly. "*We'll* be in touch. The Orchid House looks like a good property. It will fit in well with the other Donovan resorts."

Adam nodded. "I think so."

"I have to admit, in the beginning, I wasn't so sure." A wry smile twisted Warren's lips. "I thought you just liked it because of the greenhouse atrium."

"It's what first caught my attention." His voice was tight. "You have to admit it's an unusual feature."

Warren and Anne exchanged a look. Anne nodded encouragement.

"You know, son, it's hard for me to relinquish control."

Adam laughed. "A little."

"But I want you to know . . . you do an excellent job for Donovan Enterprises, Adam. I'm proud of you. But I've been thinking that with the economy slowing, we might hold off on expansion for a while. Sit back and take stock of our existing properties. Which will leave you without a position."

Did that mean Warren wanted him to cease negotiations with the Orchid House? Work in the corporate offices? Not sure if he was surprised or downright shocked, Adam started to speak, but was cut off by Warren. He was ready to defend his recommendation that the Orchid House become part of Donovan Enterprises.

"After this current project, of course. I like the Orchid House, and if things continue as they have, you might want to consider becoming manager here. Permanently."

Adam decided what he felt was shock. Warren was offering him his own hotel. A few weeks ago, he would have thought his father was trying to bury him out in the Pacific, far from the other Donovan properties. But he realized Warren was trying to give him something he thought would make him happy.

And it might.

Because the hotel was right in Jade's backyard. And it boasted a huge orchid greenhouse and one of the best tropical gardens he'd ever seen.

Anne gave him a shy smile. "Jade is a lovely girl, Adam. You would make a most suitable couple, especially as head of the newest Donovan resort."

Adam shook his head, wondering if the newly engaged couple was trying their hand at a bit of matchmaking.

"Whoa," he said with a laugh. "You two are *way* ahead of me. I like Jade. A lot. But that doesn't mean I'm ready to settle down. And I don't know how she feels about me."

He noticed that Warren and Anne exchanged a knowing look. Did they know something he didn't? But it was more than that.

"I don't know if what is developing between us will last for a lifetime. Everything has happened so quickly. I'm used to taking stock, considering options."

"Yet our ventures don't necessarily move slowly," Warren stated. "Sometimes you go in and approve a property very quickly."

Adam shrugged. "Sometimes timing is everything."

"Don't think that timing isn't important in relationships, Adam." Anne offered her warning gently. "In fact, it may be even more important than in business."

Adam took in her quiet advice. Since he hadn't shared his career crisis with them, he couldn't explain that it was a difficult time for a relationship. And neither Anne nor Warren knew how Warren's success made it hard for him to meet women who were interested in Adam himself. Or how close he'd come to marriage with Natalie the year before, only to discover she was just another female after the Donovan name and fortune.

Adam suspected that Jade was different; but he had lingering doubts. It could be that she was using him for reasons other than money. Their numerous discussions about swim with the dolphins programs came to mind. Did she really like him, or was she using their friendship to advance her environmental views?

Adam pushed such thoughts aside to enjoy the last few minutes with his father and Anne. He liked Anne more every time he saw her and he felt sure his father would be very happy married to her.

As Adam watched them wave from the other side of the security gate, his thoughts returned to the hotel. He was eager to return. Eager to walk by the dolphin pool, eager to see who might be working. Since she did so much work with the visiting school children, he thought Jade might work more on weekdays. But someone would be working at the dolphin pool, even on a Saturday, and he was anxious to see who it would be. If it was Jade, perhaps he could talk her into having lunch with him again. The thought had him smiling as he walked out to his car.

Sundays at the Kanahele household were days of relaxation. The family attended church together in the morning, then headed home for a leisurely brunch. Afterward, they read the newspaper and talked about the previous week. With both her sisters gone, Jade made a point of going home on Sunday whenever she wasn't working.

So on the Sunday following Adam's swim with the dolphins session, Jade was stretched out on her parents' couch, reading the Sunday comics. Carol had made pancakes, scrambled eggs, sausages and Spam for brunch, serving it alongside mango bread, Portuguese sweet bread, and banana bread. Jade suspected her mother was spending a lot of time in the kitchen so that she would not feel lonely in the suddenly empty house, as she always seemed to have a lot of baked goods on hand these days.

"Are you sure you don't want another piece of mango bread, Jade?" Carol stood in the kitchen doorway, wiping her hands on an embroidery trimmed towel. "It's the first batch this year."

Jade looked up. "No thanks, Mom. I'm stuffed. Best breakfast I've had in ages."

Carol frowned. "I suppose you don't bother when it's just you."

Jade thought it better not to comment. Her mother

182

probably would not approve of the toast and coffee that was her normal breakfast fare.

"I'll just pack up the breads and you can take them with you."

Carol turned back into the kitchen, her back straight with purpose.

Jade and her father exchanged a look and a smile. He was deep into the business section of the paper, she noticed.

"Jade, you'll want to read this article." He gestured to something on the front of the section. "It's continued inside. It's about the Orchid House being bought out."

Jade sat up quickly, dropping the comic pages to the floor.

"Does it say that Donovan Enterprises is buying it?"

"Pretty much." Her father handed her the newspaper, a sympathetic expression on his face that made Jade feel nervous. "It would be best if you just read it yourself. And remember, not everything you read in the newspaper is entirely accurate."

Jade took the paper.

When she finished the article, she skimmed through it again, just to be sure. Then she let the newspaper drop to her lap, and stared out the window. But she was not seeing the trees out front or the neighbor's house across the street. She was deep within herself, wondering if it was possible she could be wrong about Adam. There was real pain in her gut where her mother's delicious food now felt like a hard stone—

one of Pele, the volcano goddess's red hot stones, in fact.

Was Adam really the nice guy she'd imagined him to be? Or a businessman out to make a profit at any cost?

Jade hurried into work on Monday morning, but the usual sparkle was gone from her face, replaced by a forehead creased with worry. Would Adam come by? She'd thought of calling him at the resort, but decided she needed to speak to him face-to-face.

An afternoon and evening of serious but confused thinking had not brought her to any conclusions. And when she'd finally dropped into a restless sleep, she'd had that same troubling dream—of the ocean turning from blue to white, and herself tumbling beneath the water with nary a dolphin to help.

She'd barely stepped onto the deck when Tami and Ryan pulled her into a huddle.

"Did you see the article in yesterday's paper?" Tami asked.

Jade nodded. She felt sure everyone at the resort had seen it by now.

"I told you we had to watch that Donovan guy," Ryan said.

"Where do you suppose the reporter got his information?" Jade asked, ignoring Ryan's rant.

"It sounded like he'd interviewed Adam," Tami said.

Jade thought so too, but that did not fit in with the Adam Donovan she had come to know.

"It really doesn't seem like something he would do—provide all that information while he's still working with the hotel, I mean. I've been seeing him for two weeks and I haven't been able to get *any* information out of him. He keeps his cards close to his vest during negotiations."

Tami and Ryan remained silent. The clicking of the dolphins and the soft swish of the water lapping the deck were the only sounds.

"And that bit about the swim with the dolphins program," Jade continued, "and how profitable it could be for the new hotel. We've talked about that, and I'm sure he doesn't feel that way."

"Are you sure he wasn't just saying what he thought you wanted to hear?"

Tami's question irritated Jade.

"Of course not." But doubt crept into he r voice.

Jade's forehead furrowed in thought. "Do you think the reporter was speculating, or that someone told him they would actually be doing it?" She wanted to be fair. "Some of the other new programs sounded good."

"Yeah," Tami agreed. "I love the wedding chapel thing."

Ryan wasn't interested in the other projects.

"This isn't a tabloid rag we're talking about here. It's a serious newspaper with a good business section. I can't believe they would print an article that was all speculation on the part of the reporter. Not unless they billed it as a column. And this was a news item."

Everything Ryan said was true, but Jade hated to

lose faith in Adam. It was bad enough that she doubted him, thought that he might have provided the reporter with information. Jade knew that things were often reported incorrectly, so she wanted to hear his side before deciding if he was a bad guy after all. So far she'd held on to her loyalty for the Adam she knew.

Questions still unanswered, the three marine behaviorists entered the pool to begin the day's work with their charges.

Jade wanted to be cool and businesslike when Adam appeared, but her body, so attuned to his, betrayed her. Late in the morning, that infernal prickling on her neck let her know that he must be present.

She turned her head, and saw him approaching the lagoon. Her heartbeat kicked into overtime, and it took extra effort to fill her lungs. Tall, tanned, incredibly good-looking, Adam stepped up to the wooden railing. Expensively dressed in tailored slacks and a polo shirt with the designer logo, he looked good enough to eat.

It might be just as well that she become disillusioned about him, Jade thought. He was way beyond her touch. His clothes alone probably cost more than she made in a week. Maybe even a month.

Jade finished speaking with the group of children from the resort's day camp. She'd told them about dolphins and allowed them each to enter the shallow water and feed a fish to Laka. Now she stood at the edge of the lagoon, watching them line up to leave.

The water lapped gently over her feet, but she barely noticed. Adam kept his eyes trained on her, a brooding expression on his face.

Undecided as to whether or not to approach him herself, Jade remained where she was, waving to the children as they walked back toward the hotel. Being close to Adam was always a problem. There was so much chemistry between them, she couldn't always think straight when he was beside her.

Adam took the decision out of her hands. As soon as the children passed, he stepped around the barrier and walked up to her.

"Jade, we need to talk." His eyes bore into hers, as though willing her to believe in him. His voice was sincere. But there was a hard look to his jaw that did not comfort her.

Jade was equally serious. "Yes, we do, Adam."

She really wanted to hear his explanation of that newspaper article. She was trying hard to keep faith with him, but while the reporter had not definitely stated that the information came from Adam, the implication was there. And, as Ryan had pointed out earlier, it was a respected city newspaper, not a supermarket tabloid.

"Can you have lunch with me?"

There was no pleading in his voice today, no sexy overtones. This was his business voice, professional but firm, and more command than request.

Jade looked over at Tami and Ryan, both busily pretending not to notice the two of them.

"It would be the best way to talk without interruptions," he added.

Jade nodded firmly. "I'll get away. Tami and Ryan will cover for me if necessary." They were as anxious for explanations—and reassurances—as she was.

"Come up to my suite. I'll order lunch in. It will give us more time to talk. And there will be no interruptions."

Jade wasn't sure she wanted to be alone with him in his suite. Not that she thought his intentions were anything but honorable. Adam was being too abrupt, too professional.

"Okay. Tell me your room number."

Jade breathed a sigh of relief that she sounded normal.

Adam relayed the information she needed and promised to have lunch ready when she arrived.

"In an hour?" he asked.

Jade nodded. She watched him leave, then hurried over to report to Tami and Ryan.

Adam turned back for a final look at Jade before he entered the hotel building. She was huddled together with the other Dolphin Life workers, and there was little doubt they were having a serious discussion.

Adam's mouth drew into a tight line. He knew that article would cause all kinds of problems, knew it as soon as he saw it Sunday afternoon.

First thing this morning, he'd been on the phone with the head of the newspaper in Honolulu. The reporter had filled the article with his own suppositions, making them sound like material he'd gained from his interview with Adam. An "interview" that had consisted of one phone call and about two sentences.

Adam had the satisfaction of knowing the man would be soundly berated, and he obtained the promise of a retraction. But he was cynical about those. Numerous people would have already seen the original article featured in the Sunday paper. He doubted even half that number would notice a small retraction inserted in the midweek paper.

As soon as he ordered their lunch, he'd call the Donovan Enterprises lawyers. Exploring the possibility of a lawsuit might have some effect on both the reporter and his newspaper. Part of the concessions he'd received were probably due to his opening statement that his lawyer would be in touch.

Adam was irritated with himself. He hadn't slept well, worried about Jade and how she would feel toward him after she read the article. And he knew she would have read it. Jade's good opinion of him was of paramount importance.

At least she was willing to talk to him.

He pushed open the door and stepped into the lobby. The glass panels that delineated the orchid greenhouse from the main lobby shimmered before him, calling to him. Perhaps a short detour, before he returned to his room.

The pleasant memory of a lunch hour spent with Jade touched him. He recalled that she'd rushed to the garden when she needed time to recuperate after a trying morning.

A smile brushed his lips. They were alike in several ways, and this was one of them.

Adam stepped inside the glass-paneled doors of the greenhouse, breathing in the damp, humid air. The smell of earth and orchids was strong. Blooming plants were everywhere, and the colorful sight restored his spirits faster than anything else could have.

Except perhaps Jade. Adam realized that she had kept faith in him. While she was anxious to speak to him, there had been no shouting, no tears—none of the theatrics he'd come to expect in women when they felt betrayed by a man.

After the tenor of the previous day's newspaper article, Jade had every reason to be angry with him. The reporter made it sound as though Adam had assured him that Donovan Enterprises would increase the guests' access to the dolphins, and he knew how she felt about that!

Adam stopped before a magnificent *Vanda sanderiana*. The blooms were large, the color exquisite, but he barely saw them. Jade believed in him, he was sure of it. The thought revitalized him, even more so than the beauty of the blossoming stem of orchids.

Breaking into a smile, Adam walked quickly through the rest of the greenhouse, anxious to access the lobby he needed to get to his room. Cymbidiums, dendrobiums, cattleyas, phalaenopsis, and vandas became a colorful blur in his peripheral vision. It was a measure of his interest in Jade that he didn't notice them. All he could think about was how soon she would arrive at his door.

Jade's footsteps slowed as she neared Adam's room. Her mind was in turmoil. In her heart, she felt that Adam Donovan was a considerate man who would look at all sides of any issue. She'd spoken with him about swim with the dolphins programs and how bad they could be for the animals involved. He'd been sympathetic, had seemed anxious to learn as much as possible.

Or was she just seeing her own prejudices in him? Her own hopes? Was her newly discovered love for Adam coloring her thinking?

She stood outside the door for a full minute before she finally raised her fist and knocked.

The door opened immediately.

Adam greeted her with a somber smile.

"Right on time. Come in."

Jade had never been in one of the Orchid House suites. Adam waved her into a surprisingly large room with breathtaking ocean views. But, of course, potential buyers would rate the very best of rooms, she thought.

She couldn't resist the view and moved quickly forward to see the lovely prospect. To her delight, lunch had been set up on the balcony beyond the glass doors.

She hesitated for only a moment before sliding the door open and stepping outside.

"May I?" she called over her shoulder, as she disappeared across the threshold.

Adam watched his guest as she stepped up to the balcony railing. He smiled to see her appreciation of the unsurpassed sight available from this height.

"Beautiful, isn't it?"

He'd stepped outside quietly, standing just behind her. His voice was soft and he spoke close to her ear, causing her to jump, to turn her body into his.

Adam caught her close as she stumbled over his foot. His arms closed around her, and he could feel her warmth. He didn't know if she still wore a swimsuit, but for their lunch she'd donned a pair of denim shorts and a "Save Our Planet" T-shirt. The lettering on her shirt was faded, the cotton soft beneath his hands. The heat of her body warmed him through it, and he could feel the vibrations of her heartbeat, increasing rapidly as he continued to run his hands up and down her back. She felt so good.

Before he could lower his head to steal a kiss he badly wanted—badly *needed*—Jade broke away. She stepped up to the table, moving to the chair opposite him, her hands grasping the rounded tube that formed the upper edge of the chair back. Her knuckles whitened as she gripped the plastic and he heard her deliberate intake of breath.

"I guess we should eat. We only have an hour."

Her voice was falsely bright, and Adam cursed

inwardly. He didn't think she was ready to condemn him unheard, but perhaps she wasn't as sure of him as he'd hoped. He would try to take his cue from her.

"Let me help you with your chair."

Jade almost jumped aside as he moved around the table to pull out her chair. But his reward was a soft smile and a murmured "*Mahalo.*"

As he took his own seat, he uncovered the dishes on the room service cart and handed her a plate.

"I probably should have asked what you wanted, but I've seen you eat a club sandwich, so that's what I ordered."

Adam poured them each an iced tea from a carafe on the cart, giving her a crooked smile as he set the tall glass beside her plate.

Jade once again murmured her thanks, taking a bite of her sandwich before looking up. She patted her mouth with her napkin before fixing her gaze on Adam.

"Did that reporter interview you about the purchase of the hotel, Adam?"

Adam put down his sandwich. "That's what I like about you, Jade. Straight to the point."

He took a sip of tea while he organized his thoughts.

"I knew that article was going to cause problems. And it has, and not only with you. The phone has been ringing all morning."

Adam threw an irritated look toward the suite, where, right on cue, the phone rang. He ignored it.

"To answer your question, I did speak to him. He

heard I was here scouting the property for Donovan Enterprises. I told him that's exactly what I was doing. That's all I told him. I said it was too early to say more.

"The man obviously did his homework because all the things he said about existing Donovan properties was correct. But everything else he said about the Orchid House came from his own imagination. He certainly didn't get any of it from me." His voice hardened. "I don't talk about properties under consideration."

Jade gave a short laugh. "I can testify to that."

She wasn't smiling, but the sadness was receding from her eyes. The food lay between them, untouched.

His voice softened. "I knew you would be upset the minute you saw that bit about swimming with dolphins." He frowned. "I just hope you kept faith with me, Jade. We'd discussed this, after all, and I think you know me well enough by now to know I wouldn't just go ahead and implement a program of that kind. At least not without checking it out thoroughly."

Jade's eyes narrowed and a line creased her forehead.

"You mean you would consider such a program?"

"You misunderstood what I said, Jade. I would check into all aspects of any program being considered for one of our resorts. I would check into financial issues, of course, but I would also look at the environmental impact and speak to experts in the field."

Her hand lay on the table, and he reached for it. She pulled it quickly into her lap, making Adam frown.

"In the case of the swim with the dolphins program, I've already consulted an expert."

His direct gaze left little doubt who that expert was.

"I have it on good authority that dolphins become stressed if forced to interact with too many people and can develop health problems."

Jade's expression was softening.

"In fact, I've already spoken to Father about looking into the situation at the resort in Florida. He and Anne plan to stop there on their way back to the Virgin Islands."

Jade flew up from the table and raced around it to hug him. She even rewarded him with a swift kiss, then retreated to her own side of the table just as quickly.

"I knew there must have been more to the story." Jade flashed a brilliant smile at him as she picked up her sandwich. Her appetite apparently restored, she took a large bite.

Adam too began to eat.

"I've been on the phone with the newspaper. The reporter refuses to identify his sources, of course. I suspect it's because there weren't any. I think he made most of it up. It didn't take much to get the editor to agree to print a retraction, for all the good it will do."

Jade's happiness was undiminished.

"I thought the wedding chapel was a great idea. So did Tami."

Adam nodded. "I think so too. But that's just one of many things I have in mind for helping the hotel increase occupancy rates. As I said, the reporter did his homework. Everything he mentioned as a possibility for the Orchid House is a part of one of the existing Donovan Enterprises resorts. But I haven't taken any steps to implement any new activities. I couldn't, of course, until the resort was safely in the hands of Donovan Enterprises. It's possible some of the local managers released information anonymously. It's not difficult for them to figure out what I may have in mind from the direction of my questions. And the usual practice is to fire all managers when a new hotel takes over."

"That seems harsh. But I can see how it might cause someone to try to get back at you by leaking information—especially since you're so secretive yourself."

"It's just smart business practice to eliminate all the old guard. But at Donovan Enterprises, we try to hold on to the exceptional people. That's how I met Anne, you know. She was one of the lower managers at a hotel I was examining on Virgin Gorda."

"I've traveled in the Caribbean, but I'm not sure I know Virgin Gorda."

"It's in the British Virgin Islands, as you probably realize. Our resort there is wonderful. Perhaps you'll have a chance to see it one day."

He could see the skepticism in Jade's expressive face, but he merely smiled.

His lips twitched with mischievous delight as he

realized that the Virgin Gorda Resort would be a great place for a honeymoon. With Jade, of course.

The thought surprised him enough that he laid down his sandwich before he choked on it. Was he shocked at the idea of marrying Jade, or just surprised by it?

Before Adam could decide, Jade brought him back to the Orchid House balcony with a question.

"So was she fired when Donovan Enterprises took over?"

"No. In my report, I recommended she be kept on, perhaps even as general manager. That's what happened, by the way. She's still general manager there. And from the looks of it, Dad has been spending a lot of time there too."

"They make a very nice couple."

"I think so too."

Jade pushed aside her now empty plate, exclaiming when Adam pulled a tray of desserts from the lower shelf of the cart.

"Come on and have something," he urged. "I got one of every chocolate item on the menu. Most women love chocolate."

"It's not that I don't like it . . ."

She gestured to her stomach. There was nothing wrong with Jade's figure, and she could stand to gain a few more pounds. She was in great shape, lean and muscular. A bit more fat would only add to her slender curves.

"Go on. You'd look good with an extra pound or two."

"You sound like my mother," Jade muttered, but she did take a cup of chocolate mousse.

A soft sigh of pleasure escaped her lips as she savored her first taste. Jade took a great deal of pleasure in the treat. It was one of the things Adam loved about her—the way simple pleasures gave her so much joy.

One of the things he loved about her?

Adam put down the half-eaten chocolate chip cookie. He loved Jade?

Coupled with his earlier thoughts of a honeymoon, this new idea sent him reeling. He was almost certain Jade had been using him and his apparent interest in her to lobby for her beloved dolphins. But her reaction to the newspaper article seemed to indicate a deeper trust of him than he would have expected.

He was so deep in thought, he almost missed Jade's question.

"So," Jade asked, her spoon rattling as she dropped it in the now empty mousse cup, "now that you're fully thirty, how do you feel? Should I have gotten you a cane? A walker?"

Chapter Eleven

Amusement danced in Jade's eyes as she teased him about his birthday.

The jesting nature of the question was just what Adam needed to pull himself out of the whirlpool of questions swirling in his mind.

"It feels good, actually." He smiled, but the smile drooped as he looked at her pretty face. She was so much more than a pretty face. "You've been a good influence on me, Jade."

So much for a lighter mood, he mused. But he did want to let her know what a transformation he'd gone through in the past two weeks.

"I've been thinking about my career and my promise to my mother. I don't think I told you this, but I changed my major after she asked me to. On her deathbed she made me promise to go into my father's business."

A strange noise issued from Jade's throat, and he paused. But she did not say anything and he continued.

"I've come to realize that it really wasn't fair of her, making me promise something so important while she was dying. She knew I'd agree just because it would make her happy and that I would follow through because of my promise to her. But now I realize, her first loyalty was to my father, and she was ensuring that *he* would have what he wanted."

"Oh, Adam."

Jade's eyes were sad, and he was concerned that some of that might be pity. There were a lot of emotions he wanted to stir in Jade, but pity wasn't one of them.

"It's all worked out. I like working in the family business; there's a real pride involved when you work for a company that was started by your father. And I know that I'm contributing to its continued success."

Jade's brilliant smile teased his lips into a response.

"These last few days with Father have been a revelation. For both of us. We haven't spent a lot of time together in recent years—actually not since Mother died, because I left for college right afterward. I always competed with him and I'm sure that didn't help our relationship."

"Plus your resentment for being coerced into the company," Jade said quietly.

Adam appreciated her understanding.

"I was determined that I would prove that not only could I do the job he had done, but be better at it."

Jade reached for his hand and held it between both of hers. The affection evident in the action made his heart feel light.

"I also came to the realization that I do love what I do. Part of it is family pride, but that's okay too. And you were right. Providing people with the means to enjoy themselves is important. Everyone needs a chance to relax, to recoup their inner strength and reserves. Providing them with wonderful facilities to do that is a special calling. And that's what we do."

Jade smiled. "I'm glad. Everyone should—"

"—love what they do," they finished together.

For a moment they sat at the table, comfortable in the silence of the moment, holding each other's hands. Birdsong and the rhythmic sound of ocean waves provided a natural form of mood music.

Finally Jade spoke.

"Tomorrow's my day off."

Adam smiled. "Is that a hint?"

Amusement gave his classic features a softer appearance. He seemed more approachable, and definitely ready for fun.

Curious about this new side of Adam, she postponed the invitation she'd planned to offer.

"I'm glad you're feeling more comfortable with yourself."

Adam seemed surprised by her statement. He'd probably anticipated an invitation to spend time with her the next day. Well, she'd get to that.

"I'm glad too."

Adam ran his fingers down her cheek and she wondered if he could feel her shiver at the light caress.

"And I owe a lot of it to you, you know. Though the time I spent with my father was a turning point for us. We talked, but not about business. We got to know each other again."

"I'm glad. You seem like a happier person."

"I feel that way too. A lot of the problem was the situation at my last location. There was a general feeling among the entire management staff—part of the culture there, I think—that I had gotten my position by birth rather than performance. Add to that the takeover situation, the possibility of job losses, and the fact that my Spanish could be better. By the end, I'd proven to them all that I knew the business as well as, if not better, than any of them. But it always rankles me when people believe the worse of me, and it's happened over and over again."

Jade's heart ached for him. "I think you've been lonely."

Jade's quietly voiced words hit Adam with the impact of a falling coconut. He frowned. Lonely? Him? He was always surrounded by people, wherever he happened to be working. Could get a date any night, or day.

Except here it had been different . . .

"Having your father here eased the loneliness for you."

And you did too, Adam thought.

He didn't want to consider it, but the truth hit him hard. He moved often, didn't make many friends at the new locations because he was often viewed as the enemy. He'd learned early that those who did offer friendship usually had ulterior motives.

In Mexico, though, it had been different. An old friend of the family had a retirement home in the area near the resort where he was working, and they invited him over often.

At first, the dinners and parties provided a welcome diversion from the stressful situation at the hotel.

And then he'd met Natalie. The niece of his friends, she was beautiful and loved to have fun. He thought he was in love, until the real Natalie showed through the sophisticated veneer. She'd wanted him to return with her to spend the Christmas holidays in San Francisco. Her family entertained lavishly at Christmastime and she wanted to show him off. He pleaded work and she'd had a tantrum, screaming that he didn't *need* to work, that his family had plenty of money. She wanted him to stop pretending to work and spend more time playing with her.

It had been a painful lesson, but Adam felt glad to have been saved from her clutches. He'd actually planned to propose that Christmas.

However, the debacle had dealt a severe blow to his perception of women and their motives. He'd thought Natalie a safe bet as someone who loved him for himself. After all, her family had as much money as his. Maybe more. But she'd turned out to be a child interested only in self-gratification and the image she projected to her important friends.

His voice was thoughtful when he finally replied to Jade. "You may be right."

Jade nodded, apparently satisfied that he considered her seriously. Then she glanced at her watch. Adam checked his Rolex.

"I guess you have to be getting back."

"Uh-huh." She sighed.

"About that day off you have tomorrow . . ." he reminded her.

Jade smiled. Not only did her lips turn upward in a charming fashion, her eyes twinkled at him. "If you don't have other plans, I'd love to take you to a beach I know in Kealakekua."

"The one the wild dolphins visit?"

"You remembered."

Jade wondered if that was love that shone from his eyes. She had such tender feelings for him, but had no idea how he felt about her. Except that he seemed to enjoy her company, as he continued to ask her to join him for lunches and other outings.

Now he lifted her hand, looking into her eyes. Mesmerized, she stood before him, staring into those beautiful eyes, while a warm serenity flowed through her. Was it that the blue of his eyes evoked an image of the blue underwater world? She's always loved the twilight atmosphere of the ocean.

"Would you like to come with me?" Her voice came out in a near whisper. There was such emotional intensity filling the air between them that it seemed to smother the volume of her words.

"I can't think of anything that would give me more pleasure."

His voice too was soft. But then he broke the bond between them by flashing her a mischievous smile.

"Well, maybe one thing."

Jade laughed, but she could feel her cheeks tingling from the heat of her blush.

"I'll pick you up—" she began.

But Adam was shaking his head slowly back and forth.

Jade interrupted herself, giving him a questioning look. "What?"

"You live between the hotel and Kealakekua, don't you?"

"Yes."

"Then it makes no sense for you to come for me. Give me directions to your place and I'll pick you up.

You can drive from there if you'd rather." He squeezed the hand she'd almost forgotten he still held. "I have to tell you, though, that I've done a lot of driving since I've been here, so I know my way around the island fairly well."

Jade explained how to find her condo. "Don't you want me to write it down for you?"

"No, I have a good memory for this kind of thing. I'll find it."

"Okay. I'll see you tomorrow then."

Jade smiled. Adam lowered his head. Jade watched his eyes move closer, saw her face reflected in the clear blue of the irises. His breath feathered over her forehead, then her cheek. Her eyelids grew heavy, drooping over her eyes as he finally reached her lips.

He touched his lips softly to hers, a bare illusion of a touch. His cheek brushed hers, cool and slightly rough with his emerging beard.

Just as Jade thought she could go on doing this for the rest of the afternoon, Adam pulled back, resting his cheek against the top of her head.

Jade's ear pressed against his chest and she could hear the steady thumps of his heartbeat. The *rapid,* steady thumps of his heartbeat. It was good to know that she was not alone in her reaction to his kiss. Because it had been beyond special for her. She couldn't be sure how it had affected him emotionally, but she did know that physically at least, he'd liked it a lot.

Jade leaned her head back so that she could look up at Adam.

"That was nice."

Adam chuckled. "Only nice?"

"Maybe real nice."

He laughed. "Okay. I thought so too. In fact, it was so nice, I think it's time to say good-bye. I'll see you tomorrow."

He leaned down to place a light kiss on her lips. A light kiss that rapidly became another soul-wrenching exchange. Finally, he pulled away with a groan.

"Past time to say good-bye," he muttered.

Jade had to smile at him. Her heart was so full, she couldn't keep a solemn face on the moment. He was so considerate, he was thinking of her. Of her feelings, of her family. That she had to get back to work. He might belittle the word *nice,* but that's what he was. It was a good word, a good descriptive term.

"I really like you, Adam Donovan."

His eyes brightened at her words.

"And I like you, Jade Kanahele."

With a final wave, she walked from the suite and strode rapidly toward the elevator.

Jade decided to sleep under the quilt again. She wanted to give Grandmother Helen another chance to "talk" to her.

The dream came just before she woke. And for the first time she remembered it clearly.

It started the way the dream usually did. She was swimming in the ocean, swimming with wild dolphins. It was wonderful. A dozen sleek animals moved around her. The peace flowed through her, the happiness of being one with nature.

Then the water began to churn. She was floundering, being pulled down into a strong current. Just as she began to panic, the undertow released her. Slowly, she began to rise. The white, roiling water calmed, turning beautiful and blue once more.

Finally, Jade broke through the surface of the water. She was able to breath again, fell into the easy pace of swimming again. Serenity flooded her system, flowing slowly from her heart, out through the rest of her body. The world was beautiful again.

But there was something slightly different about this swim. There was no echolocation, no tingling as the sonar rippled through her.

She looked around her.

The dolphins were gone. But there beside her, matching her stroke for stroke was another swimmer. A large swimmer.

Jade realized that the swimmer was Adam at the same moment she awakened. She was no longer uncertain about her dreams and their meaning. This time she knew Helen had spoken to her—had meant to speak to her. Helen had let her great-great-granddaughter know that she would find the same peace and serenity she found with the dolphins in Adam. Her ancestor had confirmed her choice, had acknowledged her love of him.

Jade jumped out of bed, a big, happy grin on her face. Today would be the final test. How would he react to swimming with the wild dolphins? Teddy had done it, but only because it was the latest "in" thing. He didn't feel the tremendous strength of the dolphins, the sacrifice they made to allow human contact. Adam's reaction would be the key to whether or not they would be able to connect.

It was a beautiful day. To get the necessary early start, they'd left before dawn. The sun rose over the mountains behind them as they drove the narrow twisting road down to Kealakekua Bay. Even with his need to concentrate on the difficult road, Adam was able to appreciate the beauty of the morning. This was going to be a special day.

Now safely out of the car, Adam looked up at the pristine sky, so clear and blue it hurt the eyes to see it. A paltry few puffy clouds marred the expanse of azure, and a sliver of white moon hovered near the horizon.

Adam gazed out over the ocean. It too had joined in the conspiracy to make this day perfect. Calm, as blue as the sky, the surface of the water rippled with soft movement. There were no whitecaps, no wind, no waves to make their swim a potential danger.

Adam smiled inwardly, glad that things were coming together so well. He wanted the day to be perfect. It would be a good omen for all that he hoped would follow.

On the drive from Kona, Jade lectured him on the etiquette of swimming with dolphins. However, it had taken nothing away from the enjoyment of the drive. In fact, the sound of her voice was part of the pleasure of the morning.

Kealakekua Bay was an area of unbelievable natural beauty. The sheltered bay was the spot where Captain Cook dropped anchor in January of 1779, where he was greeted as a reincarnation of the god Lono, and where he died a month later in an altercation with the natives.

"The Bay is a protected marine area now," Jade told Adam. "There's great snorkeling there, but today I'm hoping to see dolphins."

Her happy smile turned sad, though, as she spoke of the danger faced by the area.

"It's these ecotourism packages that have become so popular. Bed and breakfasts are popping up all over, and more and more groups and individuals are coming in. Everyone wants to interact with the dolphins these days." She sighed.

Adam knew she was right. In his online research on the Big Island, he'd uncovered numerous agencies willing to bring people to Kealakekua Bay to swim with the dolphins. Such tours on a daily basis had to have some effect.

When he said as much, Jade eagerly agreed.

"They're doing a study now on how all this interaction with people might be harming the spinner dolphins. But we do know that they are not coming into the bay as often as they used to. In the seventies, the dolphins came into Kealakekua Bay on seventy-four to seventy-nine percent of the days each year. In the mid-nineties, the number of days had decreased by twenty-five percent. During the time between the two studies, there was a tremendous growth in the number of people coming into the bay for swim with the dolphins activities. And there are more and more people coming all the time. It's sad."

Now, as they sat on the small rocky beach at Napo'opo'o preparing their snorkel gear, Jade continued to instruct him on technique.

"Don't approach or chase them. If you just kind of float, they'll usually come up on their own. That's their way of inviting a human to join them."

Adam nodded. He couldn't resist a smile. He felt like one of the children she instructed at the hotel.

As they approached the water, awkward in their flippers, Jade peered toward the entrance of the Bay.

"Look." She pointed out to sea. "Here they come."

Adam saw the leaping, spinning dolphins just as others on the beach did. A cry went up, and everyone rushed to enter the water. Luckily, it was early, so the Bay was not as crowded as it would be later. Less than a dozen others were present.

They eased into the warm water, pausing to set their masks in place. Behind them the towering cliffs rose, before them the smooth blue water stretched all the way to Japan. And the exuberant dolphins were entering the Bay, ready for some play before their rest period.

Adam was excited. How could he not be? Jade had

done this many times before, and she was excited. He could feel the energy sizzling through her at the anticipation of her swim. It was inevitable that he would catch that expectancy from her.

He swam through the cool blue world of the ocean—Jade's world. The Bay was crystal clear, and teeming with life. Colorful tropical fish glided through the water and Adam noticed a sea turtle swimming away at their approach.

Some hundred yards out, Jade signaled him to stop. Together, they floated, watching the dolphins approach. Now that he was no longer moving, Adam could hear the squeaks and clicks of the dolphins. He felt a strange tingling sensation, and realized he was feeling the dolphins' sonar as it traveled over and through him.

The pod they'd seen approaching looked like a large one. Impossible to tell from the water how many animals might be in it, but the leaping, spinning dolphins covered a fair area, indicating a large pod.

Then Adam saw a few animals break from the larger group and swim toward them. Three of the large animals began to swim lazily around, then under him.

Adam noticed Jade swim slowly forward, so he did the same.

Although he'd been leery of the descriptions Jade offered, he was suddenly aware of the magic of the moment. The large sea creatures, swimming, jumping, and leaping around them, were actually allowing him, a mere human, to join them in their world. Not trained animals, held in captivity and relying on humans for their food, these wild creatures were nonetheless inviting them to visit and to play. The realization made him feel indescribably special.

The dolphins led them into a game of tag. They swam ahead, then leaped from the water, spinning in their unique way. They seemed to be urging the humans to follow as they slowed their progress, then they would repeat the whole performance.

After some time at this play, Adam found himself swimming alone alongside one of the large animals. Almost as long as he was, the dolphin was keeping pace with his slower strokes. As he turned his head to the side, Adam looked right into the eye of his companion. Intelligence and curiosity gleamed from the dolphin's large brown eye. And fun.

With a quick movement, his swimming partner moved to the side, caught a large, flat, floating leaf on his nose—his rostrum, Adam corrected himself—and brought it over to Adam.

The dolphin flipped the leaf from his rostrum to his pectoral fin, then released it as he passed by Adam. The leaf floated over the water between them, and Adam grabbed hold of it.

Jade had told him of this little game the dolphins played and he felt honored to be chosen to participate. He waited for the dolphin to make another pass, dropping the leaf in his turn. His new friend grabbed it up once more, swimming rapidly away, the large leaf riding on his rostrum.

The interlude with the dolphins was so special, Adam lost all sense of time. When the animals put some distance between them and seemed ready to settle into their rest period, he glanced around.

Jade floated nearby, watching him. With hand signals, they agreed to swim together back to the beach.

The Bay was becoming more crowded. As they left the water, Adam noted the clutter of kayaks and swimmers. A wide-bodied catamaran was anchored farther out, probably the source of many of the swimmers now in the water.

As they showered off, Jade had some pithy comments to make on the actions of a few kayakers who were chasing the dolphins—a practice prohibited in the marine preserve area.

But by the time Adam turned off the water, she was back to more personal topics.

"Are you tired?" Jade asked, shaking her head to clear the hair from her eyes. Crystal droplets of water flew off her hair, sparkling around her like fairy dust before allowing gravity to pull them to the ground.

Jade had released her hair before rinsing off beneath the showers, surprising but delighting Adam. He loved her hair when it hung free. It curled around her head in untamed tendrils after their swim, shining from the dampness of the water, shimmering with diamond-like drops that still clung to the long strands.

She looked beautiful.

Adam swallowed hard as desire engulfed him. He let his hair drip into his eyes, instead securing his towel quickly around his waist. Unfortunately, Jade began rubbing her hair with a towel, eliminating those attractive and appealing droplets.

He finally turned his mind away from Jade and her ministrations to her hair. Was he tired? Not at all.

"I should be tired." He glanced at his waterproof sports watch. "Do you realize we were out there for over an hour?"

He shook his head. "It was an incredible experience. Do you ever lose the wonder of it?"

Jade shook her head. Unfortunately, there were no more diamond-like drops of water, but Adam was still hypnotized by the long wavy strands. He could definitely imagine himself handling that wonderful mass of curls. He would love to bury his hands in it, slide them along her scalp and through the strands.

Adam pulled his mind back to the Bay. He forced himself to look at the rippling water, at the other people, anywhere but at Jade and her fascinating hair.

Jade was answering his question. "I'll never lose the wonder of swimming with wild dolphins. Each time is as special as the first. Each time is a little different. They are wonderful creatures, aren't they? Now you know why I feel so passionately about saving and protecting them."

All Adam's efforts to relegate his mind to mundane topics flew out the window with her mention of her private passion. He'd seen her passion for her pet projects, her deeply felt concern for the sea creatures she so loved.

"They're a lot like you, you know."

Adam looked from Jade to the dolphins, some of whom were still leaping and spinning out of the water.

"Or maybe you're a lot like them." He reversed the comment with a smile, as his gaze moved back to Jade. "That sense of fun, their exuberance for life— those are the same qualities you have."

Jade didn't think she'd ever received a nicer compliment.

"Why, thank you, Adam. What a nice thing to say."

And now she knew for sure. Adam was the man she'd always hoped to find. The fact that his family had money didn't matter. Their different backgrounds didn't matter. The important thing was that they experienced things in a similar fashion. And that they respected each other's thoughts and opinions.

"At one point, as I was swimming, I turned and looked right into the eye of one of the dolphins. And he looked so smart, so full of fun. I got the feeling he was laughing at me, floundering along with my inefficient little arms and legs."

Adam rubbed a towel over his head, shaking it in wonder at the same time. "I'll never forget it."

Jade smiled at Adam and she felt sure her love must be spilling from her eyes. Did Adam know how much she loved him? Sharing this experience with him was so special. And it had been like her dream. The two of them swimming together in the ocean, and the total peace they found with the dolphins, remaining with them as they swam back together, just the two of them.

"Did you feel the peace?" Jade asked.

"Actually, I did."

She watched as Adam smiled sheepishly at her.

"I thought all that stuff you said about your experiences swimming with the dolphins was just so much New Age mumbo jumbo. It's what a lot of these people are looking for."

He gestured out toward the Bay and the numerous people now swimming there.

"But I was surprised. Because I could sense the power in the dolphins. They're large, and there's a lot of vigor and strength in them. Yet they allow puny humans to join them, even invite them to play their games. I felt special when that dolphin dropped his leaf beside me."

Adam actually looked embarrassed.

"My heart did some silly thing that I would never be able to explain to anyone else—and that I'll deny forever if you tell," he added with a fierce stare. "But there he was, as big as I am—bigger weight-wise, I'm sure. And he was just being friendly, having fun, asking me to have a little fun too."

Jade didn't know what to say. She took Adam's hand, squeezing it tightly in both of hers. Together, they walked back to the rocks where they had left their gear.

The silence was comfortable. And probably just what was needed. Adam wanted time to assimilate all that had happened, all that he'd felt.

They remained locked in their thoughtful quiet until they reached the car.

"Where to now?" Adam asked. Jade had put a cooler in the car but had not said where they might go for a picnic. "I thought we'd have our picnic here, but that was before I saw the place."

Jade chuckled. "No, not here. I thought we'd go over to Pu'uhonua O Honaunau. It was a place of refuge at one time and is a National Historic Park now. Have you been there?"

"No. I heard about it, of course, when I was exploring the island's attractions. But once Father arrived I didn't do as much traveling around. I'd like to see it."

Jade was enthusiastic. She wouldn't try to sell Adam any more "New Age mumbo jumbo" but she got the same glow of serenity there as she did in the water with the dolphins. It was a very special place—the area where ancient Hawaiians headed when they broke the law, the old *kapus*. If a *kapu*-breaker could gain access to the small peninsula, he was given sanctuary. The only access was from the sea, however, across a shark-infested bay. But once there, certain rituals were performed, then the *kapu*-breaker was free to leave without penalty.

Perhaps it had to do with the fact that it had always been considered a sacred area. There were the remnants of two *heiaus* there, plus a reconstructed temple where the remains of ancient and revered chiefs had once been kept.

But whatever the cause, Jade found the spot a wonderful place to regroup, to meditate, or just to picnic.

"I think you'll like it. It's a beautiful spot, and it's usually quiet there. You can hear the birds sing, hear the waves break. I love it."

"Then I'm sure I'll like it too."

They spoke of their experiences with the dolphins on the drive to the park. Jade was anxious to hear all the details of Adam's swim, what he'd done, how he'd felt. She was glad he'd driven after all, so that she could devote her entire attention to watching him and listening.

Jade first took Adam on a quick tour of the Pu'uhonua O Honaunau site, then they chose a picnic spot and settled down.

Jade spread her quilt, an old *kihei pili,* to the side of a tall coconut palm where there was shade and a soft padding of grass. Unlike the beautiful appliqué Hawaiian quilts her grandmother made, the *kihei pili* was a typical patchwork piece, rows and rows of brightly colored tropical prints sewn together and lined with flannel. Jade had been using this particular quilt as a picnic or beach throw for years and the original brilliant colors of the fabrics had faded to a comfortable, almost pastel pastiche of Hawaiian prints.

They didn't talk much during their meal, just enjoyed the food and the scenery and their memories of the morning with the wild spinner dolphins. The day continued fine, though clouds were gathering.

"It will probably rain soon," Jade observed.

Adam grabbed at an empty paper chip bag that the wind tried to take from them.

"I guess that's our cue to clean up."

He made short work of putting the remnants of their picnic back into the cooler. They remained where they were, however, lounging on the quilt with soft drinks, listening to the sound of the ocean and the chatter of the birds.

Adam reached across the short distance between them to take Jade's hand.

"This has been quite a day. And it's only half over."

He stared at their joined hands, at the swaying shadows of the palm fronds creating patterns over them.

"Swimming with the dolphins was the most incredible experience of my life." His gaze moved upward until their eyes met. "I'll never forget it."

Jade couldn't help her smile. It was the same silly one she'd worn going in to work on that first morning, when their eyes met across the narrow stream of the lagoon and energy crackled between them.

"I knew you'd like it."

"It's more than that. In just two weeks, you've changed my life completely, Jade. With your Pollyanna outlook . . ."

Adam stopped speaking as Jade frowned mightily at his use of the hated term.

He smiled at her before continuing. "Okay. With your *sunny* outlook, you've made me face up to my life, evaluate what I have and what I want. And I want you."

Jade blushed, hoping he meant what she thought he did.

"I love you, Jade Kanahele. I think I fell for you the day our eyes met across the room—that night of the reception at the Orchid House."

Jade was thrilled. She thought she'd fallen for him then too. Grandmother Helen would be so happy.

To her surprise, Adam shifted so that he was now on one knee before her. He looked into her eyes, taking her hand in his.

"Jade, will you marry me?"

Jade's smile was so wide she felt sure she looked ridiculous. Yet how perfect could this be? Some women might dream of a proposal by candlelight, with roses scenting the air, and herself all dressed up with perfect makeup and hair. But Jade didn't care about all that. Here, in her swimsuit, a pareau knotted at her chest, her hair wild and sticky with salt, the ocean scent and sound . . . she even thought she could hear the call of wild dolphins. *This* was perfect.

She pulled Adam toward her.

"Yes."

She leaned forward, trying to reach his lips. Adam helped. The kiss was as wonderful as always.

Jade grinned. "There's a tradition in our family that the women are very good at picking their men. Good men."

"I hope so."

"There hasn't ever been a divorce."

"Good."

"I plan to uphold the tradition." She flashed another grin.

"*Mahalo.*"

Her heart melted to hear him thank her for loving him.

Jade flung her arms around Adam's neck. Someday she might share with him the story of the other family tradition—the Lovell women's legacy. But for now, she just planned to keep that "New Age mumbo jumbo" to herself and enjoy its fruit.

Epilogue

"Ladies and gentlemen, may I present the new Mr. and Mrs. Adam Donovan."

Jade and Adam Donovan smiled at their family and friends as the organ soared into the familiar strains of Mendelssohn's "Wedding March" from *A Midsummer Night's Dream.* Equal parts applause and tears followed the newlywed couple as they stepped from the altar and started down the aisle.

For this, its first wedding, the new wedding chapel at the Orchid House resort was decorated with trailing azure ribbons and hundreds of white orchids.

As the organ music temporarily quieted to a smoother part of the melody, Carol and Frank followed the wedding party from the chapel.

"Jade was beautiful," Carol said.

"Yes, she was."

"And you look wonderful in your tux." Carol's look

spoke of love as rich now as on their own wedding day.

Frank smiled into his wife's eyes. His hand closed over hers, resting lightly on his arm and he leaned over far enough to place a quick kiss on her lips. But a momentary concern sobered his expression.

"Do you think Jade will be happy with him?"

Carol's smile was confident. "Of course. You heard her explain about the dreams. Grandmother Helen brought them together." She gestured at the happy couple, posing for the photographer. "Look at them. They are very much in love. And you've heard Adam say how Jade has changed his life for the better. I think Grandmother Helen saw two lonely souls and managed to put them together."

Frank shrugged without comment, his eyes on the group at the front of the chapel. His gaze moved from Jade to her maid of honor.

"Will Jade be passing the quilt on to Momi now? This is the first time there has been more than one daughter to give it to."

Carol didn't seem concerned. "I told Jade she should keep it for now, sleep under it sometimes. Momi won't be finished with her schooling until next May. That's some five months from now. I don't think we should depart from the tradition of giving it to the next woman in line until she finishes her education."

Like the two lovebirds they still were, Frank and Carol held hands as they watched their daughters standing together at the altar while the photographer snapped pictures of the wedding party. Jade had asked Momi to serve as maid of honor and Ruby to be her one bridesmaid. Both of them wore sky blue dresses that floated and rippled like the nearby sea.

"Do you think we'll be having another wedding this time next year?" Frank grinned as he asked the question, his arm tightening around his wife's shoulders.

Carol rested her head against his chest. Her lips parted in a sweet, knowing smile. "It's certainly possible. Very possible."

Center Point Publishing

600 Brooks Road ● PO Box 1
Thorndike ME 04986-0001 USA

(207) 568-3717

US & Canada:
1 800 929-9108
www.centerpointlargeprint.com